W9-CAJ-112

Jealous Rage . . .

"Don't!" Longarm pleaded, raising his hands and wondering how he could get to his own six-gun hanging in its holster off the back of his little dining room table. "Odell, as you well know, I'm a federal officer and that means that, if you kill me, you'll hang. If you even wound me, you'll go to prison for at least ten years. Is that what you want? Huh?"

Odell barked a crazy laugh while his eyes darted around the apartment. "I been to prison before and I can take it."

"I'm sure you can, but why go through that hell?" Longarm asked, trying to keep calm, which was difficult because Odell Crabtree was a crazy and dangerous man. A man that would go to any length to save what he considered to be his honor.

"Stand back," Odell warned, going over to the bed and dropping to his knees in preparation for peering under it.

Longarm saw what was his one and only chance to survive. Odell's next look would be in the closet and he'd find Etta cringing in there for certain, and then he'd go into a killing rage and both he and Etta would die. So Longarm lunged at the huge man while he was starting to peer under the bed and used the top of his bare foot to kick Odell in the ribs with all of his might.

Odell grunted and collapsed for an instant. Then the incensed husband twisted around and raised his gun. But Longarm had thrown himself across the room and was grabbing his own pistol from its holster.

"Odell, don't!" Longarm shouted, knowing in his heart that the big man was going to do his damnedest to kill him. "Don't . . ."

DON'T MISS THESE
ALL-ACTION WESTERN SERIES
FROM THE BERKLEY PUBLISHING GROUP

THE GUNSMITH by J. R. Roberts

Clint Adams was a legend among lawmen, outlaws, and ladies. They called him . . . the Gunsmith.

LONGARM by Tabor Evans

The popular long-running series about Deputy U.S. Marshal Custis Long—his life, his loves, his fight for justice.

SLOCUM by Jake Logan

Today's longest-running action Western. John Slocum rides a deadly trail of hot blood and cold steel.

BUSHWHACKERS by B. J. Lanagan

An action-packed series by the creators of Longarm! The rousing adventures of the most brutal gang of cutthroats ever assembled—Quantrill's Raiders.

DIAMONDBACK by Guy Brewer

Dex Yancey is Diamondback, a Southern gentleman turned con man when his brother cheats him out of the family fortune. Ladies love him. Gamblers hate him. But nobody pulls one over on Dex . . .

WILDGUN by Jack Hanson

The blazing adventures of mountain man Will Barlow— from the creators of Longarm!

TEXAS TRACKER by Tom Calhoun

J.T. Law: the most relentless—and dangerous—manhunter in all Texas. Where sheriffs and posses fail, he's the best man to bring in the most vicious outlaws—for a price.

TABOR EVANS

LONGARM

FACES A
HANGMAN'S NOOSE

JOVE BOOKS, NEW YORK

THE BERKLEY PUBLISHING GROUP
Published by the Penguin Group
Penguin Group (USA) Inc.
375 Hudson Street, New York, New York 10014, USA
Penguin Group (Canada), 90 Eglinton Avenue East, Suite 700, Toronto, Ontario M4P 2Y3, Canada
(a division of Pearson Penguin Canada Inc.)
Penguin Books Ltd., 80 Strand, London WC2R 0RL, England
Penguin Group Ireland, 25 St. Stephen's Green, Dublin 2, Ireland (a division of Penguin Books Ltd.)
Penguin Group (Australia), 250 Camberwell Road, Camberwell, Victoria 3124, Australia
(a division of Pearson Australia Group Pty. Ltd.)
Penguin Books India Pvt. Ltd., 11 Community Centre, Panchsheel Park, New Delhi—110 017, India
Penguin Group (NZ), 67 Apollo Drive, Rosedale, North Shore 0632, New Zealand
(a division of Pearson New Zealand Ltd.)
Penguin Books (South Africa) (Pty.) Ltd., 24 Sturdee Avenue, Rosebank, Johannesburg 2196,
South Africa

Penguin Books Ltd., Registered Offices: 80 Strand, London WC2R 0RL, England

This is a work of fiction. Names, characters, places, and incidents either are the product of the author's imagination or are used fictitiously, and any resemblance to actual persons, living or dead, business establishments, events, or locales is entirely coincidental.

LONGARM FACES A HANGMAN'S NOOSE

A Jove Book / published by arrangement with the author

PRINTING HISTORY
Jove edition / December 2010

Copyright © 2010 by Penguin Group (USA) Inc.
Cover illustration by Milo Sinovcic.

All rights reserved.
No part of this book may be reproduced, scanned, or distributed in any printed or electronic form without permission. Please do not participate in or encourage piracy of copyrighted materials in violation of the author's rights. Purchase only authorized editions.
For information, address: The Berkley Publishing Group,
a division of Penguin Group (USA) Inc.,
375 Hudson Street, New York, New York 10014.

ISBN: 978-0-515-14870-1

JOVE®
Jove Books are published by The Berkley Publishing Group,
a division of Penguin Group (USA) Inc.,
375 Hudson Street, New York, New York 10014.
JOVE® is a registered trademark of Penguin Group (USA) Inc.
The "J" design is a trademark of Penguin Group (USA) Inc.

PRINTED IN THE UNITED STATES OF AMERICA

10 9 8 7 6 5 4 3 2 1

If you purchased this book without a cover, you should be aware that this book is stolen property. It was reported as "unsold and destroyed" to the publisher, and neither the author nor the publisher has received any payment for this "stripped book."

Chapter 1

Deputy United States Marshal Custis Long was thinking that he needed to take up a new and more financially rewarding profession. It wasn't as if he didn't find being a lawman challenging and filled with adventure and excitement, but more and more he was feeling rather like a pauper living from one day to the next. His landlord had just raised the rent on his apartment by ten dollars a month and the price of heating coal had sky-rocketed so that he'd had to pinch pennies just to stay warm this past hard Colorado winter. Furthermore, he needed to replace his wardrobe because his frock coat was frayed at the sleeves, the seats of his pants were shiny from wear, and his boots were worn down so far at the soles and heels that the local cobbler swore they were beyond repair.

But worst of all, Longarm had lost a fair amount of money lately playing poker, which was usually his additional source of revenue. This had reduced him to eating less meat and more beans and potatoes, and lately he'd been drinking a brand of cheap whiskey that was agitating his stomach and giving him the trots. Oh, and finally, the price of his favorite cigars had almost doubled in the last year and he detested smoking cheap cigars.

How long had he been a deputy United States marshal? He had stopped counting. But his pay hadn't really gone up all that much, while the prices he paid for everything kept rising month after month.

"For years I've been helping the rich get their money back one way or another," he muttered as he prepared to go out for a Sunday stroll along Cherry Creek to clear his mind and perhaps lift his spirits. "But while I've been helping the rich get richer, I've been getting steadily poorer. And the truth is that I'm not getting any younger."

Longarm stood in front of his mirror and appraised himself. He had to admit he still cut quite the dashing figure. He was well over six feet tall and ruggedly handsome, if women were to be believed. But he knew that if he wasn't killed in the line of his duty as a federal marshal, he was going to lose his looks someday, and when he did, he didn't want to be old and living on charity or handouts.

Longarm pulled his old coat on and settled his flat-brimmed brown hat firmly on his head because it was breezy outside. This was March, typically one of the windiest months in Denver, and today was one of the nicer days they'd had in weeks. A man needed to get his exercise and fresh air after a long, snowy winter, and that was exactly what Longarm intended to do this morning.

As he stepped out the door, his landlady, Mrs. Etta Crabtree, called, "Marshal Long, have you got my rent money this morning?"

Longarm had been hoping to avoid the woman by leaving before she or her drunken husband crawled out of their beds. But it hadn't happened and now he was stuck and trying to make up some lame excuse.

Forcing good cheer into his voice, he waved, smiled, and said, "Good morning, Etta. Fine morning for a walk, I'd say."

"It'd be a finer day if you paid me your overdue rent."

"Well, now, Etta," Longarm hedged. "I fully intend to do that."

"When?"

"Soon," he said, trying to move past her but unable to do so in the narrow upstairs hallway.

"How soon?" Etta demanded.

Longarm didn't like this badgering woman very much. Even though she had once been quite a beauty, Etta Crabtree was now pudgy and loudmouthed. Her husband, Odell, was a big mean barroom brawler who was always yelling and stirring up trouble when he wasn't off spending the rent receipts in some low-class saloon. This morning Etta wore a faded housedress and very little in the way of undergarments. When she walked, you could see everything that moved under that dress, and there was a hell of a lot moving. Longarm knew that Etta thought she always aroused him and she was interested in more from him than just rent money.

"I'll have the rent by the end of next week," he promised. "Next Friday is payday."

The landlady planted her hands on her wide hips. "Custis, you said that *last* Sunday. You probably spent your last paycheck on wine, women, and song," Mrs. Crabtree said accusingly. "I've seen you bringing those pretty young girls up to your apartment . . . never the same one, either . . . and I *know* they don't usually leave until early morning. Given as many different women as you consort with, I'm surprised you don't have a dripping disease."

"A 'dripping disease'?" he asked, unsure of what she meant.

"Sure! Cock rot! You know, the French disease." She squinted one bloodshot eye and said, "You don't have that, do you?"

"Hell no. And as for the women, well, they keep me from feeling lonesome at night."

"Yeah," she snorted, "I'll just bet they do. Some of the women that you bring up here look like they're barely out of their teens."

"Etta," Longarm said, desperately wanting to change the subject, "I could give you ten dollars this morning, if that would help."

"It would help." She stuck her hand out, palm up. "Odell spent all our money last night drinking and raisin' hell, so I'll take your ten dollars right now."

Longarm hoped that he had that much pocket money. He yanked out his wallet and counted the bills. "Sorry, Etta. Looks like I've only got eight dollars on me this morning."

"Give it to me," she demanded. "And you know, Odell is saying that I really ought to start charging you late fees every month."

"Etta, you and your husband have already raised my rent twice in the past twelve months, and if you do it again I'll be looking for a new apartment."

Longarm had used this threat before and it had lost its value. "You know that you won't find a nicer apartment for the money. And we've got the perfect location. We're near the Federal Building where you work so that on the bitterly cold winter mornings you don't even have to hail a horse-drawn cabbie, which saves you plenty of money."

"That's true, but my carpets are threadbare and . . ."

Etta Crabtree cut him off. "And haven't we been real tolerant of your bringing so many young women up here at night? How many landlords would put up with that kind of sinful behavior?"

"I have no idea," Longarm replied.

"Well, I do. *None*. There is not a Christian couple in town would allow you to do what you do with all the girls."

"I don't bother anyone, Etta. We don't make much noise."

"Hell, yes, you do! Why, I've heard women howling from your bed. I've also heard your headboard banging against the wall at all hours of the morning, and those bedsprings of yours must be shot by now; they were brand new when you moved in here."

"I could use a new mattress," Longarm admitted. "Now, Etta, if you'll excuse me, it is Sunday and I need to get in a good, refreshing walk. I have to have some exercise."

"You get all the exercise you need up on that squeaky bed."

Longarm could feel himself starting to lose his temper. "Excuse me, Etta. But I'm going for my walk now."

But as he tried to pass, she grabbed his worn coat sleeve, leaned in close, and whispered, "I *might* also be willing to forgive you the late rent, Custis. I might even be willing to show you a lot more exercise than if you went out for a walk."

Longarm feigned shock. "Etta Crabtree! Are you suggesting what I *think* you're suggesting?"

In reply, she cupped the large breasts sagging under her housedress, lowered her voice, and said in a voice hoarse with anticipation, "Why don't we go back into your apartment and see what we can do about that late payment?"

"Etta, I really don't . . ."

She pulled back and her voice hardened. "Custis, I've got two parties that are on the waiting list for that apartment. They are Odell's friends. They want it badly, and if you aren't willing to . . . ummm, negotiate a mutually satisfactory settlement with me . . . well, then . . ."

Etta left no doubt in Longarm's mind what was necessary if he wanted to keep his apartment. And he did want to keep it quite badly. If there was one thing that Longarm hated, it was to move. Moving was a huge bother and it was expensive. Longarm had always felt he would about rather take a beating than move all his belongings to another dwelling.

"What do you say, Custis?" Etta Crabtree winked. "My old man ain't going to wake up until noon, so that gives us a couple of hours to negotiate your rent and work out something on a more permanent basis."

"You mean like significantly reducing my rent for . . ."

"That's exactly what I mean, providing that you have met my expectations."

Longarm looked away for a moment, realizing that he really didn't have a whole hell of a lot of choice but to try to meet Etta Crabtree's sexual fantasies and expectations.

Like it or not, the walk he had looked forward to enjoying this morning along Cherry Creek would just have to wait a few hours longer.

"All right, Etta. But you're sure that Odell is going to be sleeping awhile longer?"

"He never wakes up until noon."

Longarm consulted his pocket watch. "It's ten-thirty.

I guess that gives us an hour before your husband wakes up."

"At least an hour." She licked her lips. "This could be the start of something pretty good for you, Custis. And I think I'm going to like it just fine myself."

"What about Odell?"

"He'd much rather drink and fight than screw. He once was a champion bare-knuckles fighter but he took so many punches he's never been right in the head since he left the ring."

"Is that what's wrong with him? I thought it was just that he drank himself into a stupor every night."

"That too," Etta admitted. "But precious time is a'wastin'. Let's get down to business."

"I can tell you're a real romantic," Longarm dead-panned.

"I ain't lookin' for serious conversation," Etta said, pushing him back toward his apartment. "I'm looking for some serious humping."

"Come on then," he said. "But I want half off my monthly rent."

"A third."

"Half," he insisted.

"We'll see what you got and how good you are at pleasing Etta, and then we'll negotiate. Unlock your door and shuck outa those clothes!"

Longarm backpedaled to his door, unlocked it, and started undressing on his way to his little bedroom. "Take a look at that carpet and you see what I was say-ing, Etta."

"There's only one thing I want to look at, and it's hanging over the carpet hip-high, Big Boy. Now come and let's get after it!"

Longarm quickly undressed and Etta raised her housedress over her head to reveal a voluptuous body that was all curves and rolls. If he'd been drunk, he might have thought Etta was passable, but stone-cold sober, it was going to be a stretch.

"On your back," she ordered. "Looks like you got the meat, but it's limp."

"Give me some help, Etta. You've kinda caught me by surprise this morning and I haven't had time to get my mind around this yet."

"Well, while your mind is trying to get around it, my lips are going to be getting around this!" she said, grabbing his floppy manhood and stuffing it into her mouth.

"Etta, for gawd sakes, take it easy with that!"

She answered, but her voice was muffled by his rod and while he lay fretting about what she might do to him, the feeling came that she was doing a pretty nice job of just making him hard.

"Not bad, Etta. Not bad at all."

"You ain't seen nothin' yet!"

And Etta wasn't bluffing. Five minutes later she was pounding him through the mattress, and the headboard she'd complained about earlier was banging against the wall so hard she thought that everyone in the building must be wondering if there was construction going on this morning.

"Whoopee!" Etta cried, crouched on him and hammering her huge, fat buttocks up and down like a pile driver. "Oh my gawd, this feels good!"

Longarm's eyes were big and bugged. Etta was on the attack, and she must not have had a good ride from Odell in years, given the way she was going on right now. "Wooo-weee! You make me almost want to pee!"

"Gawd, Etta, don't piss on me!"

"Oh, honey, I ain't gonna piss on you! But I'm about

to flood you with all my love juice. Get ready, here it comes!"

And true to her word, Etta unleashed some bodily fluids from her pussy that absolutely stank like a skunk. She went crazy and Longarm was trying to get his hands on his manhood before she plain broke it in half in her crazed frenzy of sexual satisfaction.

"Etta," he groaned as he expended another wad of seed and rolled off his landlady, thoroughly exhausted. "It's past noon and I'm wrung out like a dishrag. Got nothing left in me to give and that's the honest truth."

She pushed him aside and grabbed his slick and rapidly shrinking cock in her hand. "I can make this snake grow again real soon," she cooed. "I can and I will."

"No!" He tore himself out of her grasp and stood up beside the bed. "We've done it three times in less than two hours and I'm used up. So from now on I'll pay half the rent or by damned I'll find another place to sleep."

"A third."

"Half or I start moving today!"

Etta looked at his limp dick and swallowed hard. "All right," she moaned. "Your rent is cut in half. But I get you three mornings a week."

"Sunday mornings will have to do," he argued. "I have to be at my desk five days a week and often on Saturday morning, so it's Sunday morning for us or it's no deal."

"You drive a hard bargain," she said, massaging his rod in the hope of one more round, "and you also drive a real hard cock. All right. I'll just have to figure out something to tell Odell about why we're getting less rent."

"You're a smart woman, Etta. You'll figure out something."

"You bet I will," she vowed, rolling off Longarm's

bed and reaching for her housedress. "And I'll be so horny by next Sunday that it will make this morning's session look like kid's play."

Right then, Longarm knew for certain that he was going to have to find a new apartment or that Etta Crabtree might ruin him for life.

Chapter 2

"Etta! Etta, I know that you're in there! Open up, gaw-dammit, or I'll knock this door down!"

"Oh my gawd!" Etta cried, housedress falling forgotten from her hands. "It's Odell!"

"Etta, I'm coming through this door!"

Longarm looked around in a panic. His apartment was on the second floor and it was far too long a leap down to the back alley for Etta or himself. There was no way out and very few places to hide.

"Etta, get under the bed! Quick!"

"That's the first place Odell will look, and besides, I wouldn't fit!" she whimpered. "My gawd, he'll kill us."

"I got a gun and I'm gonna kill you both!" Odell shouted, banging on Longarm's door so hard it rattled on its hinges. "Open up and take your medicine!"

"Get in the closet," Longarm ordered. "You'll fit. Cover yourself up with my clothes."

"But . . ."

"It's our *only* hope," Longarm said, shoving the naked woman into his closet and closing the door. "Now let me handle this, and don't you even breathe loud."

"Odell will kill the both of us. You don't know what a temper he has and how jealous he is of other men."

"Shut up and let me handle this. I'm afraid that I've had some experience with this kind of thing before," Longarm told her as he frantically tried to get dressed.

He wasn't fast enough. Odell weighed nearly three hundred pounds and now he slammed through the door, knocking it completely off its puny hinges. He had a loaded gun in his hand and murder burned in his blood-shot and watery eyes.

Odell crouched like a dog ready to spring to the attack and growled, "My wife was seen coming into your apartment over an hour ago and nobody saw her leave! Where is she?"

"There must be some mistake," Longarm said, desperate to think of a way out of this deadly situation. "I confess that I did have a woman in this apartment this morning, but it wasn't your wife."

"Bullshit! I know that you've wanted her body from the day you first moved into this building. I could see it in your eyes! The way you looked at her body whenever she was around."

"That's not true, Odell. Now why don't you settle down and put that gun on the table so we can all calm ourselves a bit and talk about this in a reasonable manner."

"Talk!" Odell raged, pointing the gun at Longarm and cocking back the hammer. "I'll show you how I talk to a man who has just spent the last hour humping my Etta!"

"Don't!" Longarm pleaded, raising his hands and wondering how he could get to his own six-gun hanging in its holster off the back of his little dining room table. "Odell, as you well know I'm a federal officer and that means, if you kill me, you'll hang. If you even wound me you'll go to prison for at least ten years. Is that what you want? Huh?"

Odell barked a crazy laugh while his eyes darted around the apartment. "I been to prison before and I can take it."

"I'm sure you can, but why go through that hell?" Longarm asked, trying to keep calm, which was difficult because Odell Crabtree was a crazy and dangerous man. A man that would go to any length to save what he considered to be his honor.

"Stand back," Odell warned, going over to the bed and dropping to his knees in preparation for peering under it.

Longarm saw what was his one and only chance to survive. Odell's next look would be in the closet and he'd find Etta cringing in there for certain, and then he'd go into a killing rage and both Longarm and Etta would die. So Longarm lunged at the huge man while he was starting to peer under the bed and used the top of his bare foot to kick Odell in the ribs with all of his might.

Odell grunted and collapsed for an instant. Then the incensed husband twisted around and raised his gun. But Longarm had thrown himself across the room and was grabbing his own pistol from its holster.

"Odell, don't!" Longarm shouted, knowing in his heart that the big man was going to do his damnedest to kill him. "Don't . . ."

They both fired at the same instant. But Longarm was a crack shot and he was standing flat-footed and half naked in his kitchen while Odell Crabtree was down on his knees gasping from the kick he'd just received.

Odell's bullet passed Longarm's head and shattered his only window overlooking the back alley. Longarm's bullet had a downward trajectory and it smashed through Odell's thick forehead and blew the big man's brains out the back of his skull to spray across the threadbare carpet.

Etta began to scream. She fought her way out of Longarm's tiny closet, still naked, and threw herself across her quivering husband's body. "Oh my gawd, you killed him! You murdered my poor Odell!"

"I didn't murder anyone," Longarm snapped. "The man fired first and I returned fire in self-defense."

"No, *you* fired first!" Etta cried. "I *saw* you."

Longarm staggered with disbelief. "That's impossible, Etta! You couldn't see anything hiding behind my clothes in the closet."

"I *did* see. And you shot first and murdered my poor Odell!"

Longarm had trouble comprehending how this nightmare was unfolding. He was a man of action who had been in many life-and-death struggles, but this was the worst situation he'd ever found himself in, and now this fat sow was going to tell everyone that he had fired first and killed her husband out of, what? . . . Jealousy? Or the need to possess Etta?

"Listen," Longarm said as he heard the sound of running feet in the hallway. "Etta, you've got to get control of yourself. You've got to tell the truth, and that is that Odell was crazed with rage and bent on killing us *both*. Therefore, the only choice I had was to shoot him before he shot us dead! Do you understand that I just saved your life as well as my own?"

She was on the floor naked and clinging to the mass of flesh that had been her alcoholic and worthless husband. "Odell loved me and you shot him so that you could possess me."

"That is insane!"

"No, you did it!"

Longarm holstered his gun. He looked over his shoulder at three other tenants standing in the doorway and gaping at the pool of blood slowly spreading across the carpet. They were also staring at him, still only half dressed, and at Etta, whose porcine body was glued to the dead body of her husband. They had seen the gun in Longarm's fist and watched him holster it.

"Get out of here!" Longarm shouted, marching over to grab his broken door and try to close it despite the fact that it was no longer attached to the frame. "Go on!"

"We'd better call the police," one of the tenants said, nervously backing into the hallway.

"Yes," another readily agreed. "Let's get the authorities over here right now before he also kills poor Mrs. Crabtree!"

"Git!" Longarm shouted. He ran them off and then finished dressing while Etta clung to her dead husband and sobbed her heart out.

"Did you really love him all that much?" Longarm finally asked when Etta had stopped crying and was glaring at him as if he were the devil himself. "I mean, your dead husband was a notorious barroom brawler, a womanizer, and a drunken wreck of a man."

"I *did* love him! And his family is . . ." Etta caught herself up just in time and lowered her head on Odell's broad back.

"Odell's family is *what*?" Longarm asked pointedly.

"Nothing." She sobbed and began to stroke the greasy hair over one ear, being careful not to get any blood on herself. "Never you mind, Marshal."

Longarm sighed and found a bottle of cheap whiskey. He really, really needed a stiff drink. He took a long pull and sat down at his dining room table, thinking that this was about the worst Sunday morning of his entire life. "What were you going to say about Odell's family?"

"Only that they love him too."

"Where are they?"

"Boston. All the way back in Boston. Odell's father owns a manufacturing plant. We were thinking of selling this apartment building and moving back there. They are getting on in their years and we would inherit everything."

"So Odell's parents are rich?"

Etta nodded. "That's right. They are very rich and you just murdered their only child!" Etta stabbed an accusing finger at Longarm. "Mr. Dunston P. Crabtree will hire the best attorneys that money can buy, and before you know it, you'll walk the gallows for killing my poor husband!"

All at once, Longarm understood what he was really up against and it made his knees shake. Etta Crabtree would say *anything* to protect what she saw as her chance to inherit a fortune. Longarm could see Etta concocting some story about how he had forced her into his apartment, repeatedly raped her, and then shot the husband who was trying to rescue her from further debasement and abuse.

"Etta," he said, almost pleading with the lying woman, "you can't do this to me. You can't lie about what happened here this morning and how it was your idea to reduce the rent I'm paying in exchange for a good romp on Sunday mornings."

Her chin lifted and her eyes glittered fiercely. "Do you really think I'm going to tell my rich in-laws what happened here this morning and lose a fortune for honest stupidity? Do you *really* believe that, Marshal Long?"

"No," he said, suddenly feeling about a hundred years old. "I guess that I don't."

"Then at least you're not as dumb as poor Odell," she said, standing up and reaching for her housedress, then pulling it on. "How did you think people like Odell and me came to own this fine, two-story apartment building?"

"I never gave it a moment's thought."

"Well, perhaps you should have. Odell's old man bought it for us free and clear. But now that Odell is dead, they'll want me to go and take care of them as they grow old and feeble. I'll have to wipe their skinny, shitty asses in a few years and bow and scrape like a maid. But considering their money and the inheritance I'll get . . . I'll *gladly* do it. I might even figure out a way to hasten their departure."

"Maybe a little poison, or perhaps just a pillow over the face? Is that what you're thinking?"

"I'll be able to come up with something a little more clever than that, Marshal."

Longarm clucked his tongue in wonder and pity. "Etta, being the fat pig and lying whore that I now realize you are, won't you at least miss what would have been a string of great Sunday mornings here in my bed?"

She sighed. "You wouldn't have lasted long with that arrangement. I could see the shame of it in your eyes. You'd have carried out your end of the bargain for a month, maybe two, and then you'd have quit on me and moved out. But now, you won't have to worry about finding a new apartment because you'll be housed first in a jail, then in a prison, and then you will hang. So no more rent, Custis. No more rent for you forever."

Longarm knew he was looking at evil very sure of its triumph. "Don't be so quick to think I'm going to be found guilty of murdering your husband. Because what this will all boil down to is your word against mine. And seeing as how I'm a federal law officer, I like my chances."

"Mr. Crabtree's money and lawyers will put a noose around your neck and I'll start living like a queen in Boston. Remember, Custis, when it comes to what happened here, you are going to be seen as a sexually crazed man who forced me into your apartment and took advantage of me three times in less than two hours. Men will think you a vile animal to be exterminated, while women will think you are a threat to society and a betrayer of your sacred oath of office."

"So you're going to make up some wild tale to get me hanged and tell it to a judge and jury under oath."

"Damn right, I will."

Longarm pulled on his boots, strapped on his gun, buttoned his shirt and then his vest. "I'm going to be outside waiting for the local authorities. I shouldn't have to wait very long, and I'm going to tell them exactly what took place in my apartment this morning."

"You do that," she hissed, tearing the neck of her housedress, then raking her fingernails across her big, sagging breasts until they bled. "And I'll tell them how you raped me again and again like a rabid animal."

Their eyes locked, and in that instant, Longarm knew that he was in deep shit. Despite his being a dedicated and decorated officer of the law, Etta, with her torn breasts, would be the one who would garner all the sympathy of a jury.

"You're not going to send me to prison, much less the gallows," he told Etta. "Ain't gonna happen."

"You can't stop it," she crowed after sitting on his bed and smearing a little of her blood across her chest. "You might as well try to jump in front of a freight train and stop it with your bare hands."

Longarm regarded her for a moment, thinking that she was a monster. "Etta, let me ask you one question before I leave."

"Shoot."

His voice was very calm and controlled. "Did it ever occur to you that if I *am* sentenced to be hanged, I'll find a way to get free and throttle you slowly to death with my bare hands?"

Etta Crabtree paled and gulped rapidly before she threw back her head and laughed hysterically.

Chapter 3

Local sheriff Bert Belcher did not like the federal government and he especially did not like the federal law officers. In the first place, the federal law officers were better paid, better trained, and better equipped than his local constables. That being the case, whenever he did recruit and hire a really good law officer, that fellow most often left the City of Denver and went to work making considerably more money for the United States Marshals Service. And in the second place, the federal officers just enjoyed more prestige than the local authorities. They got all the big and interesting cases while his poor officers did the grunt work of hauling in drunks, petty thieves, rapists, and the general lowlifes that were always found in the core of any large city.

The really big and interesting crimes almost always went to the feds, and that was what really angered Sheriff Belcher, in addition to the fact that many years earlier he had applied for the job of a deputy marshal with the feds and they'd rejected him as unfit. Unfit! Hell, just because he'd made a few mistakes as a young man and

had once been jailed for roughing up a whore . . . And
for that they judged him *unfit*!

But now, as one of his senior officers rushed into the
sheriff's small and dingy office to loudly announce that
none other than the famous Deputy United States Marshal Custis Long had been involved in a questionable
shooting death and rape . . . Sheriff Belcher jumped out
of his desk chair with a grin that stretched from one of
his bat ears clear across his meaty face to the other.

"Did you arrest him?" Belcher cried, hurrying over to
Officer Kunkle. "Where is Custis Long?"

Kunkle immediately saw that he had made a mistake
by not trying to arrest Marshal Long . . . although he
suspected that would not have been a healthy option on
his part.

"Well, no, sir," he stammered. "I investigated the
shooting and the alleged rape of the victim, though."

"You *investigated* the fatal shooting and rape and you
didn't arrest and then put the gawddamned handcuffs on
Custis Long?" Belcher shouted in disbelief. "Why the
bloody hell not?"

Officer Kunkle was aware that the entire office was
now on their feet and crowded around him and the boss.
He gulped and tried to think of some excuse, and the
best he could come up with was decidedly weak. "Well,
sir, Marshal Long said that he killed the husband in self-
defense. And . . . and he said that he never raped the
man's wife, Mrs. Etta Crabtree. And to tell you the truth,
Mrs. Crabtree looked kinda rough."

"Rough, or roughed up?"

"Both, actually. She had scratches all over her big
tits."

Sheriff Belcher blanched with shock and outrage. "She

Manny had always said that if he ever quit the Barf squad it would only be because he was sick of defending his policies to the brass or to his own men, sick of sniping and jealousy. Though he was devoted to his family, he would never have quit for them. And never for personal safety. But Manny Lopez for the first time wondered if something wrong had happened in his own head.

Ken Kelly had always said, "Of *course* we were afraid of him. We're all afraid of psychotics, aren't we? We're terrified of unpredictable *lucky* psychotics."

Dick Snider had always claimed, "There was nobody who was crazy enough to do it except Manny Lopez."

The very last night in the canyons was by far the most terrifying of all. Everyone was secretly certain he would be murdered on the very last night. Still they walked the canyons, sweating it out to the end. Absolutely nothing happened. It was the quietest night of the year.

Manny Lopez had often said he *never* wanted it to stop. That in the BARF experiment he had found out who he *was.* But now things had changed.

Perhaps the experiment was ended not a moment too soon. Even *worse* things may have happened to all of them if they'd tried to continue the crazy experiment under a leader who perhaps had been driven sane.

had scratches on her tits and swore that Custis Long raped her and you just took Long's word that he did nothing?"

"Well, sir, Marshal Long is pretty well-respected in Denver. He's won a lot of meritorious citations for . . ."

"Bullshit on the citations, Kunkle! Don't you get it? This is finally our chance to show the high-and-mighty city fathers that *we* . . . not the feds . . . but we, the city's underpaid officers, are the ones who are on the right side of the law. And if they finally understand that, then maybe we could all get pay raises, a nice office building to work out of, and better uniforms and more respect! Did that ever enter your mind, Officer Kunkle? Even for a moment, did it not enter your mind that this was *finally* our golden opportunity to gain money and respect in this office?"

Kunkle bowed his head in humiliation. He could feel the eyes of his fellow officers boring into him with contempt. He had failed . . . but at least he was still alive and upright.

"Jaysus!" Sheriff Belcher roared in frustration. "Kunkle, are you telling me that you actually let Custis Long just walk away?"

"He wasn't walking far," Kunkle managed to say. "He lives right next to the Mr. and Mrs. Crabtree."

"Not anymore, he doesn't!" Sheriff Belcher swore. "From this day forth he's gonna live in my jail! And then he's either going to prison for murder and rape, or he's going to hang."

Kunkle raised his head. "It was Marshal Long's word against the Crabtree woman's word. It seemed pretty hard for me to believe that the Crabtree woman was the real victim."

"With her husband lying dead on the floor in their

apartment, and with Mrs. Crabtree's big tits all bloodied up, it still didn't seem straightforward, huh?" Belcher asked with derision dripping from his voice. "Are you an idiot or just a fool?"

Officer Kunkle couldn't decide.

"You're fired!"

Kunkle bowed his head even lower. The truth of it was that he had hated this job and this man who was berating him from the first day he'd signed on. He'd quickly sickened of the job of hauling vomiting drunks into this shitty little office and dirty jail cell, and one rainy and dark night a wild and huge drunk had jumped him from between two brick buildings, choked, and then beaten the hell out of him on the sidewalk. And people watching had not lifted a finger to help him! No, he wouldn't miss this job for one minute, but he had a wife and two kids to feed and he was going to have to find another job quick.

"Kunkle?"

"Yes, sir."

"I've just changed my mind about firing you," Belcher was saying. "But only because when we arrest Custis Long and he goes into a courtroom, we're going to need your sworn testimony as a town law officer to hang that big, arrogant bastard."

"But . . ."

"Don't thank me for letting you stay on awhile longer, Kunkle. In truth, I think you are one of the sorriest law officers that I've ever hired. But still and all, you look presentable and I think your testimony against Marshal Long will be looked at favorably."

"I . . . I think I'll just stay quit," Kunkle managed to say. He screwed up his courage to push on. "I'll find another job. I always kinda liked and admired Marshal Custis Long, and I don't want to testify against him when I think he was telling the truth that he didn't rape the Crabtree woman and that he shot her husband in self-defense."

Sheriff Belcher's big fist shot out and he grabbed Officer Kunkle by the throat. "You want to rethink this whole thing, Kunkle? Or do you want this office and all of us here to hound your ass until we either find you dead in some alley or . . ."

Kunkle looked around at the hard, cold faces of his fellow officers. He wasn't sure if any one of them would really do him harm, but then again he wasn't sure that they wouldn't. If they thought that he was messing up a chance for them to make more money, then who knows what they might do or say against him? Kunkle just didn't want to take the chance.

Suddenly, newly reinstated Officer Dermit Kunkle was feeling very alone and afraid. "Okay," he whispered. "I'll do it. But I still think . . ."

Sheriff Belcher pinched Kunkle's cheek so hard that it instantly brought tears to the man's eyes. "Nobody gives a shit what you think, Dermit. Not one little dog shit do we care. You'll tell me everything and then I'll tell you what to tell the judge and jury. Is that clearly understood . . . or do you want to hand over your badge and hope you make it back to that fat wife and those two bucktoothed, whiny little spawn that you call your sons?"

Kunkle was so afraid that he could barely speak. "I'll . . . I'll do whatever you say, Sheriff Belcher."

"Ah," Belcher said with a wide smile as he looked around at his officers. "Did everyone hear what Officer Kunkle just promised me?"

The officers nodded grimly.

"Excellent!" Sheriff Belcher cried. "Now I want five of you men to join me in the very pleasurable and satisfying arrest of Deputy United States Marshal Custis Long. Who will volunteer for this very important assignment?"

The officers exchanged glances; they all knew Custis Long was a hard and dangerous man. And faced with the prospect of being arrested and thrown in their stinking jail, Custis Long would be a cornered animal, and he was bound to put up a bad fight.

"None of you brave officers wants to volunteer?" Sheriff Belcher asked with sarcasm as his eyes narrowed. "What a bunch of women you sorry bastards are! You! You and you!" he yelled, pointing out the best of his men. "Get your hats and check your guns because today we are going to make the biggest and most sensational arrest in Denver history, and we'll damn sure make headlines!"

Custis Long was taking a bath when Sheriff Belcher and his officers barged through his apartment door. They caught him reaching for his Colt, and since they all had their weapons drawn and were prepared to fire, Longarm figured it only made sense to surrender.

"Belcher," he snapped. "It sounded like you and your trained monkeys busted down my door. You're going to pay for that."

"Ha!" Belcher crowed. "The only thing we are gonna be willing to pay for is a ringside seat when you hang for murder."

"Murder!" Longarm roared. "Are you out of your mind? I shot that man in self-defense. He had a gun and he fired it at me."

"Oh?" Belcher said, grinning. "According to Officer Kunkle, there was no gun in Mr. Crabtree's hand."

"What!" Longarm surged out of the tub and stood dripping and madder than a wet hen. "Crabtree even fired a shot at me."

"Is that right?" Belcher said. "And I suppose his bullet is embedded in the wall of your apartment someplace?"

"No! He missed me and his bullet shattered my window."

"So there is no bullet to be found, and no gun, either?"

Longarm swallowed hard. "There was a gun. If Kunkle didn't see it, then Etta must have snatched it up and hidden it someplace. Search our apartments and you'll find that gun, and then smell the barrel and you'll realize that it was recently fired!"

"Hmmm . . . so your defense is a gun that is missing and a smell test?" Belcher scoffed. "Marshal Long, the woman says that you raped her repeatedly and she bears the bloody fingernail marks from your hand. And to hide that bit of incriminating evidence you've jumped into a bath and no doubt washed her blood out from under your fingernails."

"Bullshit!" Longarm raged.

The sheriff's deputies cocked their pistols and Belcher said, "Go ahead and make a grab for your pistol, Long. Do it and we'll save the taxpayers of Denver the expense of a murder and rape trial."

"This is insane!"

"This is justice," Belcher countered. "And now we are going to give you the chance to put on your clothes and come down to be booked in my jail."

"The hell I will."

"Your choice," Sheriff Belcher said. He turned to his officers and said, "You all heard this man refuse to be arrested for murder and rape. Therefore, since he is resisting arrest, I order you to shoot the naked bastard down like a dog. His blood will fill the tub and the coroner will find his body has not even been touched by any of us. Case closed."

The officers who surrounded him tensed, and Long-arm knew that he was about to be shot to death. "All right," he said, so angry that he could barely speak. "I'll come with you."

"How disappointing," Officer Belcher said. "I was hoping you would just be shot all to hell and we'd be done with you."

"Someone hand me that towel."

"No," Belcher said, "get him some pants and a shirt. Then let's march him to my jail and let the fun begin."

"Belcher," Longarm said, "I don't know why you're doing this but you're going to pay for it."

"I'll like my chances," Sheriff Belcher said with a devilish grin.

"Where is Officer Kunkle!"

"He's . . . he's been sent home to rest and eat."

"He knows that what I told him was the truth. And he'll tell a judge and jury that too."

"You wanna bet?" Belcher said before he started laughing.

Chapter 4

Longarm's boss and good friend Chief Marshal Billy Vail didn't know that his best officer had been arrested until he read it in the *Denver Daily News* late the next morning. He had been sitting at his desk going over the usual boring reports that he was required to fill out and submit when his secretary, Miss Mabel Washington, came bursting into his office.

"Mr. Vail, you aren't going to like this one bit," Mabel warned, dropping the newspaper on Vail's handsome walnut desk. "In fact, it's going to ruin your entire week."

"What . . . ? Oh my gawd!" Billy whispered, staring at the headlines that read, FAMOUS U.S. MARSHAL ARRESTED FOR MURDER AND RAPE!!!

Billy Vail took a deep breath and read the front-page article quickly, then he took a few more deep breaths and read it again much more slowly. The details were sketchy, but it was plainly stated that the day before, Deputy United States Marshal Custis Long had been in his apartment with a married woman, Mrs. Etta Crabtree, who had been found nearly hysterical and with certain unmentionable parts of her anatomy violated with bloody scratches. And on the floor of the marshal's apartment was her dead husband, who Marshal Custis Long admitted to shooting twice, saying it was done in self-defense. However, no gun was found belonging to Mr. Crabtree, and the U.S. Marshal was arrested by Sheriff Bert Belcher on the charges of murder, rape, and sodomy.

"Sodomy!" Billy cried. "Why, that is ridiculous. Custis would never do such a thing! In fact, this entire article is prejudicial and misleading. Custis has been framed."

Mabel Washington was a sweet old widow and rather Victorian in her views. "I'm so glad that you said that about the sodomy, Mr. Vail. How very *disgusting!*"

"Yes, isn't it," Billy grunted, jumping out of his office chair and reaching for his hat. "I'm going down to the sheriff's office to get Custis out of that miserable little rat's cage that Belcher calls a jail cell. And after he's out, we're going to get to the bottom of this character assassination, and then we're going to find a way to get Sheriff Belcher arrested for slander! And, by gawd, I'll also make certain that the Denver City Council strips that buffoon of his badge!"

"Yes, sir," Mrs. Washington agreed. "You've never had a good word to say about Sheriff Belcher, and neither has anyone else. The man has definitely overstepped his bounds this time."

"He has," Billy Vail said as he hurried out of his office. As he passed through the larger office he could see all the rest of his staff standing up and staring at him. "Don't worry!" Billy shouted at them. "There has been a terrible injustice committed, and I'm going to get to the bottom of it if it is the last thing that I ever do!"

One of his deputies called, "I can't believe that they

accused Custis of sodomy! He's a pussy man right down to the marrow of his bone!"

"That's right," another called. "Custis would never . . . "

"Aw, shut up!" Billy yelled.

He stormed out of the office knowing that not a lick of work would be done this day, and that tongues would be wagging incessantly. Oh well, he would silence all the gossip when he got Custis out of jail and hired a good lawyer to sue Sheriff Belcher for everything he owned.

When Billy Vail slammed into the sheriff's office, Belcher was seated in his chair, feet up on his desk, reading and re-reading the day's newspaper article about what he and his officers had done the day before in arresting Custis Long. Belcher had a big cigar in his mouth and was about as happy as he'd been in the last twenty years.

"What is the meaning of this outrage?" Billy Vail cried, marching past the office staff and standing before Belcher's desk. "Gawdammit, Sheriff, you've really overstepped your authority this time. Are you out of your mind!"

Sheriff Belcher removed his cigar and blew a smoke ring that sailed lazily across his desk and broke up on Billy's chest. "What is the problem . . . *specifically*?" he asked with exaggerated innocence. "Is something upsetting you today, Marshal Vail?"

"Get your gawdamn feet off the desk and stand up and face me like a man!" Billy hollered. "I want my deputy marshal out of your jail *right now*."

"Oh, I see," Belcher said, still managing to smile. "You're talking about your murdering, sodomizing deputy, Custis Long."

Billy wanted to leap across the desk and smash in Belcher's beefy face, but he restrained himself. "You know that Custis Long would never sodomize or murder anyone, you fool. Now release him."

"No," Belcher said, dropping his easygoing pretense and standing up to his full six-foot height to look down on Vail. "I'm not releasing Long. He's going to stay in my jail until he's brought before a court and tried for murder, sodomy, and rape."

"I don't care what your grudge against Custis is," Billy managed to say. "But I will tell you this, Sheriff. When the dust has settled and all has been said and done, you're going to be finished in this town. I'm going to make sure that no one in Denver would even hire you to clean spittoons."

"Is that right?" Belcher said, his own voice quivering with anger.

"That's right," Billy Vail promised. "Now, I want to speak to my deputy marshal and I want to do it in private."

"Too bad. He's in a cell with a few of last night's drunks. I understand that, when they learned he was a law officer, they decided to take some revenge."

Billy Vail's hands clenched at his sides. Physically, he was no match in size or strength to Belcher, but he was a hard fighter and he was ready to kill.

"However," Belcher was saying, "I guess that when the fight was over, your marshal was the only one in the cell still standing. He's a little roughed up, but I suppose that he'll survive."

"Lead me to him, now!"

Belcher shrugged as if the request were of no importance. He started to deny it but then he decided that it would be amusing to see the look on this federal officer's face when he saw Custis Long bruised and battered. "Sure," he said. "I'll do it as a professional courtesy and because you asked so politely."

"Screw you," Billy hissed.

"You'd probably like to," Belcher said derisively.

Billy Vail damn near lost it at that remark. He knew that Belcher was taunting him and hoping he'd lose control and wind up getting arrested alongside his famous deputy. Well, dammit, that just was not going to happen. Billy Vail figured he was of no good use to Custis Long if he was also arrested and jailed.

"Let's go," Belcher said, seeing that his insult had not given him the hoped-for results. "I'm sure that Custis Long will enjoy seeing a friendly face. The poor bastard is in deep trouble."

Longarm was sitting on a rough iron bench that served as a bunk. Three badly beaten drunks were stretched out on the rock floor of the stinking cell. One had a busted nose, one had been forcibly made to eat his front teeth, and the last one had had his balls kicked so hard by Longarm that he could not bear to stand. All in all, they were the sorriest of chronic drunks that would have ganged up on Longarm and killed him last night had they been strong and able enough.

"Custis?"

"Billy!" Custis came to his feet and walked stiffly over to the bars. "Thanks for coming, Boss."

"I'd have come last evening if I'd have known you had been arrested and jailed."

"Yeah, I know," Longarm said, "and I asked Belcher if he would send someone to your house and give you the news, but of course he refused."

"Sheriff Belcher is in for a very bad fall," Billy said,

loud enough for the officer to overhear the threat. "Sheriff, I demand a moment of privacy with Custis."

"You're not his lawyer and you can't ask for shit."

"I'm asking you as . . . as a professional courtesy," Billy grated.

"Well," Belcher said with a leer. "In that case I'll give you five minutes with my famous prisoner. Five minutes." To emphasize his point, Belcher pulled out and consulted his brass pocket watch. "I'll be at my desk. Just sing out if you want to leave a little early, and you just might because it's really filthy and rank in here."

Billy gripped Longarm's hand through the bars and managed to keep silent until Belcher had departed.

"Custis," he said when they were alone, "you've really got your ass in a vise this time. What happened?"

"The woman, Mrs. Crabtree, came over to my apartment and . . . well, I felt sorry for her and then I screwed her."

"Because you felt sorry for her?"

"Yeah."

"But you didn't . . ." Billy could barely say the word. "You didn't sodomize and rape her, did you?"

Longarm's face clouded with anger. "You know better than to even ask that question, Billy. When have I ever had to rape a woman?"

"Never."

"All right then," Longarm said. "If the truth be told, Etta practically raped me because she wanted me so badly."

"The newspaper says that there were bloody scratches or marks on her upper body."

"She tore them across her tits after I shot her husband in self-defense."

"I see."

Longarm shook his head. "I know I messed up. I know I'm a fool and I deserve to be punished. But I am not guilty of murder or rape or that other thing I want to forget that you mentioned."

"Mrs. Crabtree claimed you done her both ways," Billy said quietly. "And the gun you say her husband fired is missing."

Longarm reached out and squeezed Billy's forearm. "You really need to find the gun that Odell Crabtree fired at me. It has to be in either my apartment or theirs."

"And what would it do to help your cause?" Billy asked. "By now, there won't be any smell of fresh gunfire. And I'm sure that Mrs. Crabtree has either disposed of it in the river or down a sewer, or she has at least cleaned it. Custis, the gun is no longer helpful for your defense."

"Then what is?"

Billy thought a moment and then shook his head. "Honestly, I really don't know. Everything points to your guilt . . . not your innocence."

"But I'm a federal officer of the law who has spent years risking his life for the good of the public!" Longarm raged. "Doesn't my record and all those commendations I've received for heroism count for *anything*?"

"I don't know. Depends on what kind of a judge that you get . . . and what kind of a jury."

Longarm let out a sigh of deep exasperation. "Boy oh boy, is this a mess. I wonder how long I'm going to have to be locked up in this shit house."

"I'm going to hire you the best lawyer I can find in Denver. I have a few names in mind. I'll hire one today and he'll see a judge and ask for a bond to be made so you can get out on bail."

"I don't have any money for bail."

"I do," Billy said. "Not a great deal, but some. And I

know that everyone in the office will chip in with whatever amount they can afford for the bail bond and the
lawyer. We'll find a way to do it."

"You're going way out beyond anything I deserve or
expected," Longarm said. "And I don't want you to put
yourself out on a financial limb that might break."

Billy blinked. "What does that mean?"

"It means," Longarm said, lowering his voice, "that if
I go to trial and am found guilty of murder and rape, I
won't go to prison for those acts that I did not commit. It
means that I'll go on the run before I'll go to prison or
walk the gallows."

Billy whispered, "And if you are sentenced to prison
or to die, then I'll help you escape. You know that, don't
you, Custis?"

"I know," Custis replied. "And I thank you for your
help and assistance."

Billy Vail looked at his finest law officer and friend
and he suddenly felt like crying. Longarm's face was
bruised and one of his eyes was swollen almost shut. "It
must have been a hell of a fight in here," he managed to
say.

"It was," Longarm admitted. "This cell is so small
that I could hardly get room enough to fend them off.
They came at me like a pack of dogs and tried to trip
and pull me down. And when I fell once, they swarmed
over me and I just went crazy. I hurt all three pretty
badly."

"They got what they deserved."

"Sheriff Belcher was hoping that they'd tear me apart.
But when that didn't happen and I beat them up, he was
so mad that he says he's also adding assault of prisoners
to the charges filed against me."

"Sheriff Belcher is . . . is going down himself," Billy said. "He just doesn't know it yet."

Longarm nodded with understanding. "We'll get him before this is over," he said. "We'll take care of him for good."

Billy looked into Longarm's eyes and a shiver went up and down his spine, because what he saw told him that his deputy marshal was going to have even more blood on his hands before all was said and done.

Chapter 5

All that day people came to pay their respects and offer their heartfelt condolences to the newly widowed Etta Crabtree. She pretended to be almost stricken dumb with incalculable grief, but inside Etta was almost bursting with joy. The death of her drunken, loutish husband had opened up enormous possibilities. She would have to stay in Denver, of course, through the murder and rape trial of Custis Long. She might even be expected to be among the throng watching him hang. Of course, she would wear the black cloth of mourning and maybe she would have to keep a little fresh onion in her purse or pocket to rub in her eyes when tears were expected. But the main thing was that she was free of Odell, and Boston's wealth was calling her into a new and much more satisfying existence.

"Mrs. Crabtree," a reporter was saying as a curious crowd stood outside of her door. "It must have been a terrible shock and ordeal that you've just gone through, and I was wondering how long you were married to your dear, departed husband."

Etta Crabtree really had no idea. She wanted to say, "Way, way too long."

"I guess it will be ten years now," she said, figuring that they'd been married about that long.

"Ten years," the reporter repeated, writing it down in his notepad. "And did you have any children?"

"Mr. Crabtree and I were never blessed that way."

"How sad," the reporter said, trying to look sympathetic.

Etta didn't think it sad at all. She *hated* kids. Couldn't stand the sniveling, shrieking, demanding, irritating little bastards.

The reporter consulted his notes and then looked up at Etta. "Forgive me for asking, and I mean no disrespect, but I understand that your husband was known to like a drink or two of an evening."

"He was," Etta admitted, knowing that her husband's wild alcoholic binges were legendary in this part of Denver. "But Odell was kind and good, and he sure didn't deserve to be shot to death. He was. . . ." She sniffled. "He was trying to protect my honor."

"But he was a bit late for that."

"Yes, he was, but he still tried. Odell was no match for a gunman like Custis Long."

"Of course not. I understand that Marshal Long is trying to raise bail and that one of the best attorneys in Denver has been hired to represent him. He says that *you* were the one that initiated the . . . the sexual encounter in his apartment."

"Me!" Etta feigned outrage and tried to dredge up a few tears for the audience but failed. "Why that . . . that sex-crazed animal raped and used me in the most vile and disgusting manner!"

"Yes, I'm sure that he did." The reporter stepped back

because Etta had not taken a bath in over a week and she smelled gamey. "You are still quite the ravishing woman, I'd say."

"Why, thank you!"

"I was wondering, Mrs. Crabtree. How do you explain the fact that the shooting, rape, and unspeakable sexual outrages took place in Marshal Long's apartment rather than your own?"

"He dragged me into his apartment."

"He did?"

"Yes. I was going out to the butcher shop when we met in the hallway. I guess he just had a sudden urge and he grabbed me and dragged me into his apartment, then closed and locked his door."

"Locked it?"

"That's right."

"And that is why your husband had to break it off its hinges."

"Exactly. Odell was no match for Custis Long as a gunman, but he was very strong. And he was so incensed that he just broke the door down when he heard me screaming for help."

"I see," the reporter said, furiously scribbling his notes. "I have heard rumors that your husband was the son of a rather wealthy Boston businessman. Is that true?"

"Yes, his dear father loved him so."

"But. . . ." The reporter looked around at the shabby apartment. "If he is wealthy and loved your late husband so much, then why would he allow you both to live . . ."

The reporter was trapped by his own words.

Etta saw that and took pity by finishing his insulting question. "Why would Mr. Dunston Crabtree allow us to live so poorly? Is that what you were going to say?"

"I . . . I didn't mean to insult you, Mrs. Crabtree, but

your circumstances do seem to be rather modest for the son of a wealthy Boston businessman."

"Odell had his faults," Etta said, choosing her words carefully. "And he would be the very first to admit that whiskey was his worst enemy. And so he made mistakes . . . like we all do . . . and he had his differences with his father in Boston. But they loved each other dearly and we were going back to Boston where Odell was determined to make sure that his father was taken care of properly in his dotage."

"You were leaving Denver to take care of Mr. Dunston Crabtree, one of the wealthiest men in Boston?" the reporter asked with obvious disbelief.

"That's right," Etta said, nodding her head. "Mr. Dunston Crabtree is in failing health and he desperately wanted us to return to his side in his last, failing years."

The reporter dutifully wrote this down. "One last question, Mrs. Crabtree, and then I will leave you to your mourning and funeral plans."

"Yes, I have much to do and it all seems so overwhelming. I can't tell you how dirty I feel after what was done to me and it is my hope that Marshal Custis Long be hanged for murdering my husband and raping and abusing me in such a shameful and horrible manner."

"My last question is, why do you think that a decorated and admired law officer such as Deputy United States Marshal Custis Long would suddenly go so . . . so haywire? Why would he commit such a heinous and barbarous act to someone such as yourself?"

"I have no idea and I don't care about his twisted inner motives," Etta snapped. "I can only admit that I've always had a strong physical effect on men . . . even though I've lost a little of my girlish beauty. Perhaps Marshal Long had been drinking or he had been fantasizing about me . . . even for months. Maybe he took some kind of *love potion* or solution that drove him into a wild *sexual frenzy*. Whatever the reason, my dear heroic husband who tried to rescue me is now dead and I have been terribly violated."

"Yes! I'm going to write that down and make sure that justice is going to be served," the reporter said. "May I use the quote of a 'sexual frenzy' possibly the result of a 'love potion'?"

"Whatever you wish to write, then write it," Etta said, now bored with this interview and wanting to share her grief with the other people standing behind the reporter.

"I will," the reporter promised. "And you'll probably be hiring your own lawyer for the trial. Have you chosen one yet?"

"Whatever for?" Etta asked, genuinely confused by the reporter's question.

"Why, not only to see that Custis Long hangs, but also to sue the United States Government because he was a federal law officer."

Etta Crabtree's jaw dropped. "I could *sue* the government?"

"I'm sure that you could if you have the right attorney," the reporter said. "It has been done before, and your case certainly seems to be one where a man who was entrusted with carrying out the law and who had taken a sacred oath of office has violated your body and taken your husband's life. Some sort of monetary consideration might be in order, I'd think."

Etta was almost dumbfounded. And elated. She didn't know if this was true or not, but it was certainly worth exploring.

"Do you happen to have the name of a lawyer who I might be able to speak to about this?"

"As a matter of fact," the reporter said, "my brother, Artemis Lanier, is an outstanding attorney and I will ask him to call upon you. My brother has a sterling record for sending murderers, rapists, and sodomites straight to the gallows."

"That's wonderful!" Etta said. "But I'll speak to him only if there is some *real* money somewhere in this for me . . . and for your brother, Artemis Lanier, of course."

"Of course," the reporter said as he smiled, bowed, and hurried away.

Chapter 6

Bail was denied and Longarm was left to await his trial in the small and filthy cell. Sheriff Belcher had arrested several big, tough brawlers, hoping they would beat the hell out of Longarm, but it had not happened.

Five days after he'd been arrested his new lawyer, Carson Elder, had convinced the judge that Longarm's life and health were at serious risk and had gotten him a private cell. In retaliation, Sheriff Belcher had cut Longarm's daily food ration in half.

"Just hang on a little longer," Attorney Elder had urged. "I've got the trial moved up and we'll be in court in two weeks."

"Two weeks!" Longarm swore. "Two weeks in this jail will seem like two years."

"I know, I know," Elder said, laying a fatherly hand on Longarm's shoulder. "But that was the best that I could do. Also, I was able to do a little backstreet negotiating and I've been able to get Judge Milton Swanson to preside over your trial."

"I've heard of him," Longarm said, brightening. "In

fact, I've testified in Judge Swanson's court a number of times and I've always thought the judge a fair and reasonable man."

"Just the kind of judge we need in this trial. He respects lawmen and I know he will give you the benefit of the doubt."

"You mean take my word over that of Etta Crabtree?"

"Exactly. Judge Swanson even had a son-in-law who was a local deputy. Unfortunately, the young man was shot to death trying to break up a saloon fight."

"So Judge Swanson is almost certain to be in our corner," Longarm said.

"I'm sure that he will be. The judge that Artemis Lanier would like to have presiding over your trail is Judge Henry Henson."

"Oh, shit," Longarm breathed. "Hanging Judge Henson is the *last* man that I'd want to hear my case. That man is full of hate for anyone charged of anything. I can't even imagine how many men he has sentenced to the gallows, and he's attended every hanging! Why, I was at a hanging where Judge Henson sent a man to death for doing nothing more than robbing and hitting a man and robbing his saddle shop of fifty dollars."

"Yes," Attorney Elder said. "If you go into that man's court you can expect no mercy or justice. I've never won a case in Judge Henson's courtroom, and I've been a defense attorney in Denver for more than twenty-five years."

"Well," Longarm said, "I'm sure glad that you were able to prevent Henson from taking my case. I've brought many a prisoner to his courtroom and I'll have to say that he was unmerciful to every last one of them."

"Hanging Judge Henson should have been thrown off

the bench years ago for incompetence. You know that cup of water he sips all during the trials in his court-room?"

"Sure. He has a big thirst."

"Yes, but Judge Henson is not sipping water, he's sip-ping high-grade *tequila*. The man is a functioning drunk."

"I always suspected that," Longarm said. "But any-way, aside from the judge, have you been able to make any headway against Etta Crabtree's slanderous and lying testimony?"

"No," Attorney Elder admitted. "She is a cow and a low-class individual, but she is smart. The first thing she did when she got her attorney on board was to learn that she should not grant me any interviews or say anything more to the press."

"So what is our defense other than my word against Etta's word?" Longarm asked with concern.

"That's it," Elder said, smiling. "But you may be sure that when I get Mrs. Crabtree on the stand I will grill her like a gawdamn mud-sucking carp . . . which she most certainly is. I'll fluster her and she'll be no match for me. Don't you worry, Custis, I'll break her down like a cheap child's toy. Bet your bottom dollar that I'll have her sobbing and admitting that *she* was the one who made the advance and that you only did her on both sides because you wanted her to reduce her rent."

"Hold on, dammit! I *never* sodomized Etta Crabtree. You got that straight, Carson?"

The attorney threw up his hands. "Yeah, sure. Don't get mad."

"Well, dammit, that really pisses me off that she'd accuse me of it, and if the jury believes her , I'm as good as hanged."

"Don't worry. Don't worry. I'll . . . I'll figure out some way to make sure that the truth comes out."

"Good. I'm counting on you. It was really fine of my boss and the people at the office to help pay your fees, and I want to make sure that the money is well spent."

"Trust me, Custis. Mrs. Crabtree's attorney, Artemis Lanier, is not my equal in a courtroom, a barroom, or the bedroom. I'll make the man look like the crowing peacock that he is and has always been."

"I'm glad to hear that," Longarm said, managing a smile. "I sure messed up agreeing to screw that woman if she reduced my monthly rent by half. I promised I'd do her every Sunday morning in my apartment while her drunken husband slept through his hangover."

Attorney Elder clucked his tongue with obvious disapproval. "I sure wish that you hadn't done that, Custis."

"Done what? Screwed Etta? Why, it was *she* who screwed me."

"No, made that Sunday morning arrangement in repayment for your rent reduced by half."

"Why?"

"Why?" Elder asked rhetorically. "Because it makes you look like a *gigolo*. A long, fat cock for hire, if you'll kindly excuse me for my bluntness. And that is not going to sit well with a jury because it will engender jealousy in men."

"Why would it do that?" Longarm asked, genuinely puzzled.

"Because by getting your rent cut in half you were effectively getting paid to screw a woman while there will be men . . . perhaps even most of the male jurors . . . who *pay* women for their sexual favors. See the difference?"

"Sure, but . . ."

"Allow me to finish," Attorney Elder said. "And because you were getting paid to screw a woman and they have to pay to do the same, then they'll obviously be envious and jealous even though they'd probably never admit the fact."

"Hmm," Longarm mused. "I'll have to think about that logic."

"It's an obvious fact of male human nature."

Longarm wanted to switch the subject. "Any chance that you can get my trial date moved up?"

"None whatsoever," Attorney Elder assured him. "But I'm going to keep hounding Sheriff Belcher about the appalling lack of your personal hygiene and care. I damn sure don't want you walking into that courtroom looking and smelling like a street derelict."

"Me neither," Longarm readily agreed. "Belcher has really been trying to put me down for the count. He's done everything he can to get me beaten to a pulp and mentally broken."

"Well, to your credit, he has failed."

"That's right," Longarm said. "I'm not one to break easy, and when my back is up against the wall, I'm a hard fighter. But I'll tell you this, Carson. When I do walk out of that courtroom and this jail a free and vindicated man, I'm going to make it my mission to get even with Belcher."

"I didn't hear you say that."

"Well, I said it and I meant it," Longarm said angrily.

Elder steepled his long, slender fingers and studied Longarm for a moment before he said, "And that would get you right back into this jail and then prison, or worse."

"I'm not a fool," Longarm said. "And I'm not the first poor bastard that Belcher has put the screws to when he was down. I'm telling you, Sheriff Belcher has to be taught a painful and humiliating lesson and he has to be stripped of all his authority."

"I agree that the man is a disgrace to his profession, but I still think that if you get even with the sheriff, it could be a very, very bad mistake."

"Mistake or not, I'll find a way to repay him. He's going to get his own dose of justice."

"I don't even want to hear about that, much less think about it," Elder told him. "Revenge is only going to bring you more grief. You are a sworn officer of the law, and you've taken a solemn oath to uphold the law . . . not take revenge on someone."

"Sheriff Belcher is not just 'someone,' Carson. He is a man who needs to get a taste of his own damn medicine."

"Let's drop this subject and talk about the upcoming trial."

"Not much to talk about, is there?" Longarm asked. "I mean, I've told you everything at least a half dozen times."

"And nothing has been left out?"

"Nothing," Longarm assured the man. "So all I can say is that I just want this damned thing over with."

"Just hang on a little while longer," the attorney pleaded. "With Judge Milton Swanson on the bench at your trial, we're home free."

"Glad to hear that," Longarm said with genuine relief. "I sure am relieved that I'm not getting sentenced by Hanging Judge Henson."

"So am I," the attorney said. "Mrs. Crabtree's attorney, Artemis Lanier, is no doubt incensed that we got the judge we wanted."

"Good! How did you manage it, if I might ask?"

"Don't ask," Carson Elder replied.

"Okay, then I won't. But thanks!" Longarm stuck his hand through the bars to shake, and when his attorney took his hand, Longarm couldn't help but wince with pain.

"What's wrong!" Carson Elder asked with concern.

"I cracked a knuckle or two in here fighting for my life," Longarm said, painfully wiggling the fingers of his left hand. "Maybe even cracked a bone in my hand. One of those bastards had a jaw like granite. I should have kicked him instead of hitting him in his thick skull."

The attorney looked stricken. "My gawd! What if Belcher manages to get someone in here and—"

"I've still got a solid right hand, my teeth, and both feet," Longarm interrupted. "You just worry about your end when I walk into the courtroom and let me worry about mine."

"I will. See you soon."

"Tell Billy Vail the good news about getting Judge Swanson," Longarm said as the attorney prepared to leave. "And thank him and the others again for helping pay your fees."

"They aren't paying *all* of them," Attorney Elder replied. "You're still going to be on the hook with me for a few hundred dollars."

"As long as you get me out of this damn jail a free man cleared of all charges, then I'll gladly find a way to pay whatever is owed."

"I know that," Elder called out over his shoulder. "If you were hanged, I'd never get my full fee."

Longarm had nothing to say about that, so he went

back to his flea- and tick-infested bunk and tried to take
a nap.

The next two weeks seemed like forever, and when
Longarm walked into the courtroom for his trial, he
was gaunt, bitter, and seething with anger. He had not
had a bath or a decent night's sleep since being tossed
in jail, and he'd lost at least twenty pounds because the
food he received from Sheriff Belcher was slop unfit
for a pig. But at least now he was going to get a fair
trial. He hoped it would be a short one and that Judge
Milton Swanson would ask for a swift and just verdict.

"Hear ye, hear ye! All rise for the Honorable Judge
Henry Henson," the bailiff called as everyone stood and
the judge entered the courtroom.

Longarm heard his attorney gasp, saw him go pale
and whisper, "Oh my gawd, it's the 'hanging judge'!"

"What happened!" Longarm whispered frantically.
"You said that Judge Swanson was going to preside over
this trial."

"He was supposed to. I . . . I don't know what happened!"

Hanging Judge Henson was a thick-set man in his
mid-fifties. He was bald and red-faced, acerbic and insulting to anyone who crossed his path. Defense attorneys actually ducked out of hallways into closets or
wherever they could hide when Judge Henson came
waddling down the corridors of the state courthouse.
The hanging judge put the fear of God in anyone who
stood accused of any crime.

Longarm could not believe what he was seeing this
morning. "Carson, dammit, what . . . ?"

Judge Henson caught the sound of Longarm's frantic
whisperings and his deep-set and bloodshot brown eyes

focused on the accused. "Is the defendant looking to insult this courtroom with his disruptive chatter? Is that what he is intent on doing before we even get started this morning?"

"No, Your Honor!" Attorney Elder cried. "Most certainly not! But . . . but we were told that Judge Swanson would be presiding here today."

"Ah, yes. Poor Judge Swanson took very ill last evening. I was called late last night and told that Judge Swanson must have gotten a very serious case of food poisoning."

"Food poisoning?" Attorney Elder managed to choke.

"Yes, I'm afraid that he is not expected to survive. I hope that is not the case, although Judge Swanson and I agree on almost nothing when it comes to the law, politics, or any other matter. But he is a colleague and I do wish him a speedy recovery, as I'm sure everyone in this courthouse does."

"Yes," Attorney Elder said, clearing his throat and trying to find a steady voice. "May I ask for a delay in this trial until we at least find out if Judge Swanson survives and is able to handle this trial?"

Henson shook his head. "Of course you may not. I've been asked to take over for Judge Swanson, and this is a rather sensational trial. I will preside over this case and you may rest assured, Counselor, that justice will be swift and fair for all."

Longarm couldn't believe what was happening. He could hear Billy Vail and several of his office workers behind him, and from the tones of their voices, it was clear that they were just as flabbergasted and upset as he and his stunned attorney were at this disastrous moment.

Meanwhile, Sheriff Bert Belcher was almost laughing while Etta Crabtree and her attorney were looking as smug and delighted as raccoons let loose in a pastry shop.

"We're really screwed," Attorney Elder said, taking out a handkerchief to wipe his perspiring face.

"There must be something you can do," Longarm whispered in desperation.

"Dammit, Custis, there is *not*."

Elder took a deep, steadying breath, and his jaw muscles tightened with resolve. Longarm's attorney was a handsome and well-regarded man in his forties. Carson Elder was a gifted speaker, had a thoughtful and impressive demeanor, and possessed a nimble mind, but right now he was so shocked and appalled at this sudden switch in judges that he could barely speak.

"Say something else," Longarm hissed. "Demand a retrial or a new judge, or we both know that I'm a dead man!"

"Your Honor," Attorney Elder stammered, coming to his feet to address the bench. "This is a very . . . uh, unusual development and we really do need some time to . . ."

"To what?" Henson demanded in a harsh tone of voice. "Would you present your defense any differently to me than to Judge Swanson? Isn't the law blind when it comes to justice? Individual differences of judgment should not have any bearing on a fair and just verdict."

"That's quite true, Your Honor, but . . ."

"But *nothing*!" Judge Henson thundered, suddenly losing his temper. "If you continue along this path of argument, Counselor, I assure you that you will not be pleasing this court. So I suggest that we begin to select a jury and get this trial underway at once."

Longarm looked into his attorney's eyes and all he saw was doom and defeat. Doom and defeat.

"I'm a dead man," Longarm said under his breath. "A dead man."

If his attorney heard this repeated and solemn pronouncement, he did not acknowledge the fact. But it was clear from the tremor in his voice that, deep down inside, Attorney Carson Elder could not have agreed more.

Chapter 7

Longarm had watched the first day's proceedings unfold as if he were watching his own funeral. The jury that was selected were all tough, uneducated working men, one of whom frequented the same saloon that Odell had favored. Longarm swore that another of the jurors was a pickpocket he had arrested more than once.

To make matters even worse, Attorney Artemis Lanier was far smoother and more accomplished in the courtroom than Longarm's attorney had led him to believe. He had brought in as witnesses the other apartment tenants who had stood outside of Longarm's broken door and observed him standing over a dead or dying Odell Crabtree. One witness after the other had recounted the gun in Longarm's fist, but no one seemed to have seen the gun that Odell had used to fire a shot at Longarm. And, of course, the bullet he'd fired had gone through the window and was therefore not recoverable.

"And you, Mr. Matson, actually saw Odell Crabtree take his last gasp of breath?"

"That's right. He was in terrible pain and suffering.

His wife was hysterical and I couldn't help but notice that her enormous ... uh ... her bosom was bleeding ... from what I could tell were scratch wounds. She looked as if she had been dragged naked through a knothole."

"Thank you, Mr. Matson, for your testimony. Mrs. Crabtree had not been dragged through a knothole ... but she had been raped and brutally *corn-holed*."

The spectators gasped with shock, and then many of them, along with the jury, began to howl with laughter.

"Order in the court!" Judge Henson shouted with a broad smile on his round and red face. He took a swallow from his glass and banged his gavel until the courtroom was silent.

"Would you like to cross-examine this witness, Mr. Elder?"

Longarm's attorney looked gray in the face but he forced himself to stand and approach the witness. "Mr. Matson, did you see any blood on Mr. Long's hands?"

"No," Matson said after a moment of reflection. "I guess not."

"But yet you say it seemed obvious to you that he had used his fingernails to ... to injure Mrs. Crabtree on her bosom."

"That's right."

"How interesting that Mr. Long's fingernails were clean and there was no sign of either blood or torn skin under them. And on another point, Mr. Matson, are you sure you didn't see a gun in Odell Crabtree's fingers?"

"I am sure."

"Could you see both of his hands?"

"Uh ... well, I don't remember."

"Then isn't it possible, Mr. Matson, that one of the hands was under Mr. Crabtree's body and that it was the one holding the pistol that he used to fire at an officer of the law?"

Matson's brow furrowed. "I suppose that's possible."

"And did you notice that Mr. Long's window was shattered and that there was glass on the floor under the sill, indicating that the damage to the window would have been very recent?"

"I did notice the broken window. It had been shattered and fell in pieces on both the inside and the outside of the room."

"Tell me, Mr. Matson, if you had a broken window, wouldn't you immediately clean up the glass so that you didn't step on it and injure your foot?"

"Well sure!"

"Of course you would," Attorney Elder said, giving the jury a long look. "And so would Marshal Long or any reasonable person. Therefore, we have to conclude that the window was broken only minutes before the shooting or even more likely *during* the shooting."

"I guess that makes sense," Matson said, almost with disappointment.

"I have no other questions of this witness," Carson Elder said. "He may be excused."

When Carson Elder sat back down, Longarm squeezed his attorney's arm and whispered, "Nice work there."

"Thank you."

Attorney Artemis Lanier was ready to call his next witness for the prosecution. "I would like next to call as a witness Denver Officer Dermit Kunkle."

Officer Kunkle slunk rather than marched up to the front of the court and was sworn in.

"He looks scared shitless," Longarm said in a small voice. "Sheriff Belcher has him by the throat and won't let go unless he testifies against me."

"I know. Let's hear what the man has to say."

Officer Kunkle squirmed in his chair as he testified against Longarm. He said that he had arrived after the shooting and seen Odell Crabtree's body but no gun in the man's hand, nor had there been a sign of any weapon at all around his person. Kunkle went on to describe in some detail how hysterical and upset that Mrs. Etta Crabtree appeared, and how her breasts had been severely raked by what were obviously Longarm's fingernails.

"Did you smell alcohol on Marshal Long's breath?"

"I did. He'd obviously been drinking."

Attorney Elder jumped up. "Objection, Your Honor. My client will admit he had a few drinks, but he certainly was not inebriated."

"Objection overruled! Your client was drinking," Judge Henson said, taking a generous sip of his tequila.

Artemis Lanier had a few more questions for Belcher's deputy, but not many. He ended by saying, "In your professional opinion, Officer Kunkle, is there any doubt that Marshal Custis Long shot to death Odell Crabtree?"

"Not a doubt in my mind."

"And would you say he did so in self-defense?"

Kunkle swallowed hard. "How could it have been in self-defense when the victim had no weapon?"

"Thank you for your testimony, Officer Kunkle. We all appreciate the fine job that you local law officers do for the City of Denver. You're underpaid and underappreciated, but I want you to know, and I'm sure that I speak for everyone in this courtroom, that we are sincerely grateful for your unfailing loyalty and service to the people of Denver."

"You are very welcome," Kunkle said, managing a boyish grin.

"He never looked at me even once," Longarm said with disgust.

"I'd like to ask a few questions of Officer Kunkle before he is excused from testimony, Your Honor."

Judge Henson scowled. "I would think that Officer Kunkle has said about all that he has to say on the subject."

"Even so," Attorney Elder pressed, "I'd still like to cross-examine the witness, as is my right by law."

"Don't you dare lecture me on the law in my courtroom!" Henson thundered.

There was a long, angry silence, but Attorney Elder stood his ground and finally Henson said, "Very well. But if your questions are frivolous or irrelevant in the eyes of this court, then I will hold you in contempt of court."

"Yes, Your Honor."

Longarm had no idea what his attorney was about to say or do, but it couldn't possibly hurt his case.

"Officer Kunkle, how long have you been on the job?"

"You mean working for Sheriff Belcher?"

"Yes, that's what I mean," Elder said patiently.

"Oh, about a year now . . . almost."

"And have you enjoyed your work and found it satisfying?"

"Uh . . . well, it has its moments."

"Then why did your wife tell me last week that you are intending to quit the sheriff's office because you can't stand to work there and you detest Sheriff Belcher and his bullying, abusive ways?"

Kunkle actually choked like a fish out of water and stammered, "I . . . I think maybe you misunderstood my wife."

"I could summon her here as a witness."

"Uh. . . ." Kunkle was frantically trying to avoid looking at his boss. "Uh . . . I may not be suited to be a deputy," he finally said. "I . . . I just think that maybe this line of work is not what I'm really cut out for."

"What do you think you are 'cut out for,' Officer Kunkle?"

"Uh . . . I'm not sure."

"Didn't you actually quit right after the shooting but then were *forced* to reconsider and remain on the job until you had finished this testimony? And before you answer that question, remember that you are under oath and have sworn to tell the truth and nothing but the whole truth, so help you God. And that, if you lie, you will be committing perjury, which is a very, very serious matter, the punishment being a substantial prison sentence."

"Objection!" Artemis Lanier shouted. "My witness is being threatened and badgered. He's a sworn officer of the law and he does not deserve such callous and insulting treatment in this courtroom."

"Objection sustained!" Henson roared. He glared at Attorney Elder. "Counselor," Henson said, his voice shaking with anger, "I also object to the badgering and threatening you have been doing to this witness who is a sworn officer of the law. And if you do so again, I will punish you!"

Longarm felt proud when his attorney raised his head defiantly and said, "Judge Henson, my client's life and reputation are at stake here. He is entitled to the full representation of the law and I intend to do just that!"

"You have been warned, Counselor. Tread lightly from this point forward or you will definitely suffer the consequences."

Attorney Elder whirled and pointed a finger at Kunkle. "Are you committing perjury?" he shouted.

Kunkle swallowed hard and looked as if he wanted to crawl through his chair backward. "No, sir!" he finally managed to cry.

Attorney Elder shook his head in obvious contempt. "You should resign your office and badge, Officer Kunkle. Your role in this farce is over and now you should just . . . just go away and hide in your shame, knowing what you have just done in this court of law."

"Objection!" Artemis Lanier shouted.

But Attorney Elder simply turned his back on the judge and prosecutor and returned to his seat with a smile grimly painted on his handsome face.

"You did the best that any man could have done," Longarm told Elder. "I couldn't have asked for more."

"You'll get more when Etta Crabtree takes the witness stand tomorrow," Attorney Elder promised. "And I don't care if Judge Henson throws me into jail with you and tries his damnedest to strip me of my profession!"

"We may *both* have to leave Denver and take up new professions before this all comes to an end."

"You're right," Elder said. "And maybe that isn't all that bad a fate, given what we are now going through."

Chapter 8

Billy Vail stopped by the jail late that afternoon and brought along a plate of his wife's fried chicken and half of a freshly baked apple pie.

"Whatcha got there?" Sheriff Belcher asked when Billy came through his front door.

"I've got a little something for Longarm's supper."

The sheriff's nose twitched like that of a hound dog on a fresh and inviting scent. "Why don't you just leave it on that desk over yonder and I'll see that he gets it later."

"No, thanks," Billy told the sheriff. "I'd prefer to take it in to him right now."

Belcher wasn't pleased. "Well, dammit, I don't care what you 'prefer.' And you'd better understand that I'm not in the habit of letting people come in here anytime they please to feed my prisoners. Hell, if I allowed that, they'd be comin' and goin' all day long and maybe even passin' along a gun or knife."

Billy detested the man but he bit his tongue and said, "Try to use your head, Sheriff. I'm the senior federal law officer in Denver. Do you really think I'd be dumb enough to bring in a weapon for my friend and deputy, Custis Long?"

Belcher shrugged and managed to look greatly pained. "Well, I guess probably not. But we have a regular schedule for feeding the prisoners, and it ain't supper time yet."

"Make an exception," Billy grated. "And please open the door so I can see Custis and give him a decent meal to eat."

Belcher groaned with displeasure and heaved his bulk out of his office chair. "I'll be damn glad when Judge Henson wraps up this trial and sentences your man to hang. Damn glad!"

"Don't you go getting that noose knotted quite yet."

Sheriff Belcher got a ring of heavy keys off a hook and unlocked the back door to the cells. "I got a hangman who is just itchin' to drop the noose around Long's neck. And I got a carpenter who is ready to throw up a gallows quicker than you could scare a black cat. Won't be long now until we do some rope stretchin', I'd bet."

Billy didn't trust himself to reply. Instead, he just motioned toward the door that Belcher had just unlocked.

"Oh, all right," Belcher said with a weary sigh. "I guess this might even count as the condemned man's last meal."

Billy hurried back to Longarm's cell. Longarm was the only prisoner in the jail at the moment, and Billy waited until they were alone. "Custis, my wife cooked up some chicken and baked an apple pie. I think you're going to like them both."

Longarm eased himself off the bench and stretched. "I sure do appreciate it, and tell your lovely wife thank you for me."

"I'll do that. How are you feeling?"

"Like crap," Longarm confessed. "I've been locked up in this cell far too long. I try to do some exercises to keep in some kind of physical shape, but there is a darkness weighing heavily on my mind and I find doing anything to be very difficult."

"Not much longer," Billy said, wanting to cheer his deputy up. "This could all be over by the end of the week."

"I'm worried about the jury that I'm facing," Longarm said. "Those fellas are gonna probably be sympathetic to Etta tomorrow. And after listening to Officer Kunkle on the witness stand, I'm thinking that things don't look too good."

"Kunkle was lying through his teeth because he is scared to death of Sheriff Belcher. Anyone with eyes could see that."

"Maybe, but maybe not."

"We're going to get you out of here soon . . . one way or another."

"Glad to hear that. Are you getting any heat about me from your bosses in Washington, D.C.?"

"Not much," Billy lied. "I've told them that you were set up on these false charges. They're not happy about the negative publicity for our department, but they know your record of service and they're standing by with their full support."

"Am I still getting paid as a federal officer?"

"Of course you are."

"Well," Longarm said, throwing his arms wide, "as you can plainly see I'm not spending much money in this gawdamn jail cell."

"When you get out I'm going to give you a long paid

vacation," Billy promised. "Maybe you can go all the way down to New Orleans and eat all that good Cajun food and fatten up a bit."

"I have lost some weight," Longarm allowed.

"Too much," Billy told him as he passed the food through a slot in the bars. "Custis, you're nothing but skin and bones. That's why you need to eat all this deep-fried chicken and all this apple pie."

Longarm snatched a chicken leg from the still-warm plate and devoured it with relish. "Mighty delicious!"

"Wait until you try that apple pie."

Longarm nodded, eating greedily. In truth he was absolutely famished for good, homemade food.

"Custis, I want to ask you something very important," Billy said, dropping his voice.

"Shoot."

"If the verdict should go against you . . . and I'm not suggesting that it will . . . are you prepared to be a man on the run for the rest of your life?"

"You mean be a fugitive rather than spend the rest of my days in prison or even worse, walk the gallows?" Longarm asked, wiping his greasy lips with the back of his dirty sleeve.

"That's exactly what I mean."

"Of course, I am."

"And you'd want to kill Sheriff Belcher, I suppose."

Longarm studied his boss's face for a moment. "Billy, for your sake, it's best that I don't answer that question."

"Your attorney has mentioned that you intend to exact revenge. That isn't surprising, but it makes things far more complicated for me and my office."

"Let's change the subject, Billy."

"Okay. But if you . . . escape with the help of friends,

then that is one thing. There will be a manhunt . . . of sorts. But you are one of us and the effort will be minimal at best, and I'll make sure that the reward for your capture will be small."

"Five hundred?" Longarm asked.

"Even less. And, Custis, you would have to change your name and go far away. Unless you really did something foolish, you would never be caught. But, if you acted foolishly and returned to this town and then killed Sheriff Belcher, then that is a whole different situation and I'd have to try my damnedest to bring you in, and then you'd almost certainly be sentenced to hang."

"I'd expect nothing less from you and the boys," Longarm said agreeably.

"So do we have an understanding?" Billy asked.

Longarm stopped eating and asked, "That being that no matter what the verdict, I won't kill Sheriff Belcher?"

"Yes. That's what I want to hear you say."

Longarm devoured a drumstick and gave the matter some very careful thought. He understood Billy Vail's situation and valued his friendship above all others. The last thing that Longarm wanted to do was put his boss in a tight squeeze. "All right," he finally said. "No matter how it goes down in the courtroom . . . no matter what the verdict . . . I won't kill Sheriff Belcher."

Billy smiled with sudden relief. "I can't tell you how glad I am to hear that."

"However," Longarm said, raising a greasy finger between them, "I just can't promise not to exact a fair measure of retribution against Belcher."

"And that retribution would be?"

"I don't know yet," Longarm admitted. "But it would be far more than just a physical beating."

"But not a killing."

"No," Longarm said. "I just promised you that I won't kill the man."

"Fair enough," Billy said with satisfaction. "That's all that I wanted to hear you say."

Longarm ate quickly and was soon done with all the fried chicken and began eyeing the pie. "Billy," he asked, belching with pleasure, "how do you think that Etta is going to look tomorrow when she takes the witness stand?"

"I think she'll look better than she has in at least ten years," Billy was forced to admit. "Her attorney, Artemis Lanier, will have her hair fixed up pretty, have makeup applied, and have Etta carefully schooled on manners and her demeanor when she is testifying. I'm afraid that Etta Crabtree on the witness stand is going to look good and sound even better."

"So her attorney is really going to doll her up for the judge and the jury tomorrow?"

"That's what Carson Elder told me. Etta's attorney has already filed against my office specifically, and against the federal government for fifty thousand dollars in damages."

"Fifty thousand!"

"That's right," Billy said. "When my bosses in Washington, D.C., got wind of the amount, they were flabbergasted and outraged."

"Has the suit any merit?"

"Not much," Billy said. "Artemis is hoping that the federal government will offer a compromise settlement of perhaps ten thousand just to do away with all the bad publicity."

"Don't let them pay Etta a cent," Longarm urged. "I'm not the one at fault."

"If you're convicted as charged of murder, rape, and

sodomy, then you will be considered the one at fault and that would be quite an embarrassment for our department," Billy told him. "So let's just see what happens in court tomorrow. I have a feeling that after Etta testifies, Judge Henson is going to ask both sides to wind up their final arguments so that the jury can make a verdict."

"I don't at all like the way this is going."

"Neither do I, but your attorney is no fool, and I'm hoping he has a few tricks up his sleeve and he'll make Mrs. Crabtree look like the liar and the greedy bitch that she really is. I can't believe that you agreed to screw that woman, Custis. I really can't."

"I can't either anymore," Longarm said, shaking his head. "But I was feeling damned poor and . . . well, I just messed up."

"That you did," Billy said. "But let's drop this whole rotten situation and talk of pleasant things like apple pie and where you would like to go after you are set free and I give you a long vacation."

"New Orleans sounds real good," Longarm told him as he used his fingers to scoop up globs of the apple pie. "But so does Old Santa Fe. I have friends in both places."

"Women friends, I'd bet."

"Women and men," Longarm said around a mouth stuffed with pie. "And I like both those cities."

"Well," Billy said, "I've never been to New Orleans, but I sure do have fond memories of the senoritas in Old Santa Fe. Not that you can repeat that remark to my wife."

"Of course not."

"I think you should go to New Orleans," Billy mused out loud. "And spend some time on Bourbon Street and maybe out in the Gulf of Mexico on a fishing boat."

"I'm not a fan of fishing," Longarm told him.

"Ah," Billy said, "but fishing in the gulf is said to be really something. We're not talking about puny little trout or bass . . . No, sir! We are talking about catching marlin and other big fighting sonsabitches!"

Longarm grinned at his boss. Sometimes Billy's imagination just got away with him, and that was always fun to watch.

Chapter 9

It was nine o'clock in the morning and the courtroom was packed and buzzing with excited anticipation of hearing Etta Crabtree's long-awaited sworn testimony.

"My gawd," Attorney Carson Elder whispered nervously. "You'd think someone famous like Calamity Jane was coming in here this morning. Or maybe Davy Crockett."

Longarm nodded in agreement. He was sitting up near the front of the courtroom and knew that Billy Vail and as many of his friends as possible were also crowded into the room and waiting anxiously.

"Carson, do you think that I'll finally have my chance to be on the witness stand today?"

"I'm almost sure of it," his attorney said. "But I'll have to tell you that the star witness of the day will be Mrs. Crabtree."

"Yeah, I know."

Just then the whispers died and the room fell silent. All heads, including Longarm's, turned around to see

Etta Crabtree being escorted into the courtroom by her attorney, the handsome and cocky Artemis Lanier.

"I can't believe it's even the same woman," Longarm said, staring at Etta Crabtree and seeing a lovely stranger.

"I can't either," Carson Elder agreed. "She looks like a stage queen instead of the lying pig that she is."

Etta's head was held high. Like Longarm but for entirely different reasons she had lost quite a lot of weight since Longarm had seen her last. Her formerly mousy hair was now colored a soft brunette and her white dress was expensive, lacy, and very proper. She wore pearl earrings and a matching pearl necklace, white shoes, and carried a sequined purse close to her side. She even walked different, and Longarm wondered how long it had taken her attorney to teach her that and if he had been forced to screw the lying cow.

Etta took a seat up front, and when she glanced sideways at Longarm there was a confident smile on her lips.

"She looks like a whole different woman than when I took her in a dirty housedress."

"She's the same woman, all right," Attorney Elder said. "We'll see if she is as composed as she looks when I cross-examine her on the witness stand this morning."

Hanging Judge Henson arrived. Everyone stood up until the judge was seated and gaveled the courtroom into complete silence. The judge cleared his throat and studied Etta Crabtree for a moment before saying, "Ladies and gentlemen, this court is now in session. I am going to first have the victim, Mrs. Etta Crabtree, take the stand for testimony and cross-examination. Then I'm going to do the same for the accused, Marshal Custis Long. After that, I believe the jury will have heard enough testimony from witnesses to recess and come back to this courtroom with a final verdict."

Longarm's attorney, Carson Elder, stood up. "Your Honor, I do have a few more witnesses that I'd like to call on behalf of my client."

"Let's hear the first witness and get on with this trial," Henson said dismissively. "Counselor Lanier, are you ready to have your client take the stand?"

"I am, Your Honor."

"Then let the bailiff swear her in."

Etta Crabtree was sworn in and took her seat. Her attorney began asking the usual questions about her background and her current living situation. He ended by asking, "And I understand that your deceased husband's father is none other than the highly successful and well respected Mr. Dunston P. Crabtree of Boston?"

"That's right. Odell's father is on his way here now from Boston. Of course, given his age and condition, he could not arrive in time for the funeral of his dear son, but he still is coming to make sure that justice is done in my late husband's name."

"Very noble and understandable," Attorney Lanier said gravely. "Now, Mrs. Crabtree . . ."

"Please just call me Etta like all my friends do."

"Very well, Etta. Could you describe for the jury and Judge Henson exactly what took place when your husband was murdered?"

"Objection!" Attorney Elder shouted, coming to his feet. "It has not been established that Odell Crabtree was murdered. In fact, *he* was the one who tried to murder my client, Marshal Custis Long."

"Objection sustained," Judge Henson growled. "Let the witness continue."

"Mrs. Crab . . . I mean, Etta, I understand that Custis Long was your tenant for approximately two years. Is that correct?"

"Yes."

"And I also understand that as of late he had been tardy paying his monthly rent. Is that correct?"

"Unfortunately, that's true, although Odell and I were very tolerant of him being late."

"But this month he was late again and he offered to pay you only eight dollars as a partial payment. Is that correct?"

"It is," Etta said, fluttering her eyebrows. "I guess that Marshal Long is quite the ladies' man and a habitual gambler. Odell and I just assumed that he was spending a lot more money on cards, wine, women, and song than he was making in his federal job."

"Yes, I'm sure that was true. Now, when he offered to pay you eight dollars as a partial payment of his monthly rent, what did you do?"

"I told him that eight dollars wasn't enough. I said I felt very sorry for him but that we had two people who were very interested in renting his apartment and in fact they would pay *more* rent. Then I asked the marshal for the rest of his overdue monthly rent."

"And what happened next, Etta?"

She sighed and her lower lip quivered. "Marshal Long, whom I had always considered a gentleman, became very angry. He cursed me and . . ."

"Wait a minute," Attorney Lanier said. "Did you say he *cursed* you?"

"Oh yes, in the most vile manner."

"That's a lie!" Longarm shouted, jumping to his feet. "I've never cursed a woman in my life."

"Sit down or I will hold you in contempt of this court!" Judge Henson roared at Longarm.

Longarm sat and his hands gripped the arms of his chair so tightly that his knuckles showed white.

"Now," Attorney Lanier continued, "I know this next part will be very difficult and require a great deal of bravery on your part, but tell us exactly what happened next."

Etta Crabtree swallowed hard and took a few deep breaths. The jury was moved by her determination to see justice done.

"Well . . . when I explained about other people wanting to rent the marshal's apartment, he just kind of went crazy. He started ranting and raving about how bad the carpet was and the mattress and he went on and on. So I agreed to go inside his apartment to see the carpet he was complaining about and the mattress in his bedroom."

Etta's voice broke. "I . . . I should never have done that, because as soon as I sat on his mattress to see why he was so upset with it, he pushed me back and . . . and he pulled up my dress and . . . oh, my gawd he did all those terrible things to me!"

Etta broke down and sobbed. Longarm groaned and realized the woman really should have been in theater. Hers was a moving performance, and a total lie.

"Give me just a moment to compose myself, please," Etta whispered as she dabbed the tears from her cheeks. "I just never had anyone do such terrible things to me before. Custis Long, as everyone can see, is a very big and powerful man. I didn't have a chance, although I fought him with every ounce of strength in my poor violated body."

"I'm sure you did," Attorney Lanier said in a voice filled with righteous anger. "How many times were you raped that Sunday morning in the man's apartment?"

"Three times."

"Three times," the attorney said slowly and with great deliberation. "And one of them was . . ."

"In my . . . my butt!"

The audience gasped in shock and horror. Longarm shook his head, knowing his fate was sealed and that he was doomed to hang.

"My dear woman," Attorney Lanier said as he comforted his sobbing client. "How bestial and depraved of a man sworn to uphold the law, of all things!"

"My dear departed husband saw him doing those dirty and humiliating things to me."

"How horrible," Attorney Lanier said, shaking his head. "And when Mr. Crabtree tried to intervene on your behalf . . . tried to save what little honor you still possessed, he was gunned down."

"Yes."

"Gunned down by a trained gunman like Marshal Custis Long."

"Objection! My client isn't a *trained gunman*; he's a United States marshal."

Attorney Artemis Lanier jabbed an accusing finger at Longarm. "One who has killed dozens of men in the line of duty, some under highly questionable circumstances!"

"Marshal Custis Long is a brave man who upholds the law!" Attorney Elder cried.

When the court erupted in shouts, the judge banged his gavel until it fell silent again. "Mrs. Crabtree," the judge said, "I know this is extremely difficult, but you need to continue so we can finish up with your testimony this morning."

"I'll try, Your Honor. So, after Marshal Long began to assault my body, my husband, Odell, must have heard my cries because he came running and then he broke down the door. He wanted to protect my honor, but he was too late! He was gunned down by the marshal. Odell loved me so much that he gave his life for mine!"

Suddenly, the door to the courtroom was flung open and a tall, elderly man with snow-white hair and a cane came limping down the aisle assisted by a large man with fierce black eyes and a powerful and imposing physique.

"Mr. Crabtree!" Etta cried, suddenly roused from her staged grief and coming to her feet. "I didn't expect to see you get here all the way from Boston so soon!"

Dunston P. Crabtree was at least eighty, but he stood ramrod straight and his face looked as if it had been chiseled from granite. He thumped his cane on the floor twice and said in a strong voice, "Etta, the sad truth is that you *never* loved my son. I didn't love my son. Odell was a wastrel, a drunkard, and a disgrace to my family!"

The courtroom was stunned. Even Judge Henson had trouble finding words. Finally, the judge said, "Sir, I must ask you to take a seat and remain silent during this sworn and difficult testimony."

"Silent!" Crabtree roared. "By gawd, I've come all the way from Boston by private coach just to attend this trial, and I'll be damned if I'm going to be silenced by some fat, half-drunk judge in a dirty black robe!"

Hanging Judge Henson had never before been spoken to in that cold and defiant manner, and he actually rocked back in his chair as if he'd been punched before he managed to yell, "Sir, you may very well be as rich as King Solomon, but I will *not* have you insulting this court. And if I hear another vile outburst from you, I will have the bailiff escort you out of this courtroom by force if necessary."

Dunston Crabtree barked a brittle laugh. "If he so much as approaches me, I'll have my manservant and bodyguard, Reinhold, rip your bailiff's arms from his body and then cram them down your throat!"

There was an audible gasp from everyone except
Longarm, who simply smiled for the first time in days.

"Bailiff, please escort Mr. Crabtree and Reinhold from
my courtroom," the judge ordered in a small voice.

The bailiff was a strong young man who could probably manhandle most troublemakers, but his jaw was
hanging open with either disbelief or fear, and he stood
rooted in place.

"Bailiff, are you deaf! Get them out of my courtroom!"

The bailiff jolted a few paces forward, and when he
got near the pair, Reinhold growled at him and clenched
his big fists. It was enough to set the bailiff backpedaling
in fear.

"Now that the threats have all been made, I suggest
we all take our seats," Dunston Crabtree told the judge.

It took several minutes for the courtroom to settle
down enough for the trial to proceed. On the witness
stand, Etta Crabtree looked as if she had seen a ghost,
and her carefully choreographed sympathetic demeanor
had slipped very badly. When her attorney resumed questioning, it was clear that Lanier wanted Etta Crabtree off
the witness stand as quickly as possible.

"All finished with my witness," he said a few moments later.

Attorney Elder stood up and walked up to the front of
the court. He glared at Etta Crabtree for a moment and
then he said, "Would you like to tell us what you did
before you met your late husband, Odell Crabtree?"

"What do you mean?" Etta asked.

"I mean, what means did you have to feed, clothe,
and house yourself? In short, how did you make a living
before meeting your late husband, Mr. Odell Crabtree?"

"Uh . . . I worked here and there at many different

things," Etta stammered, shooting a frantic look at her attorney, beseeching him for support.

"Objection," Attorney Lanier said. "The witness's past is of no concern to this murder and rape trial. I fail to see . . ."

"The question is *highly* relevant," Attorney Elder said. "And I'll show you why if the court will allow me to ask this question."

"Oh, very well," Judge Henson said, gulping down his tequila and motioning for the shaken bailiff to take and refill his empty glass. "Objection overruled."

"Then I'll repeat my question," Attorney Elder said. "Miss Crabtree, what did you do before you met and married your late husband?"

She looked up the ceiling, as if seeking guidance from above, then cleared her throat. "I was a maid in San Francisco. I worked at a millinery shop in Tucson and later as a waitress in Pueblo."

"And what were you doing in Denver before you met Odell Crabtree?" Attorney Elder moved closer to the witness until he was almost leaning over her. "Again, Mrs. Crabtree, please remember that the judge will have no choice but to hold you in contempt of his court if you lie under oath. So weigh what you say next very carefully."

Real tears formed on her cheeks. "Okay, damn you! I thought I'd suffered enough humiliation already on this stand, but if you insist on hurting me even more, then I'm sure that you somehow discovered that I was a working girl at the Red Raven House."

"Doing precisely *what*, Mrs. Crabtree?"

She tried to say it but the words just wouldn't spill from her lips.

"Then I'll say it," Attorney Elder said as he turned to

address the jury. "For almost two years before Etta met and married her late husband, she was a prostitute at the Red Raven House. And a very, very popular one. I have witnesses who will testify to that, if necessary."

"Objection!" her attorney cried.

"Objection overruled," Judge Henson said, leaning forward. "Go on with the line of questioning."

"And isn't it true that you met Odell Crabtree at the Red Raven House and he became your number one client?"

Attorney Lanier audibly groaned.

"And isn't that why Mr. Dunston Crabtree never gave his blessing to the marriage, because he knew that you were just a high-priced whore?"

Attorney Lanier objected but the courtroom was in such an uproar that no one heard him.

Longarm began to laugh out loud.

Chapter 10

Longarm was called up on the witness stand next. He had been prepared for his own attorney's questions and was answering them smoothly and convincingly. "And finally, Marshal Custis Long, did you rape, sodomize, or in any way do physical or mental harm to Mrs. Etta Crabtree?"

"No. My only fault was in being foolish enough to accept her offer of giving me a greatly reduced rent for making love to her."

"And when her husband broke down your door?"

"I felt ashamed of myself," Longarm admitted. "I tried to reason with Odell Crabtree and calm him down, but he was out of his mind and wasn't hearing anything I said. Moments before he'd busted down my door, I hid Mrs. Crabtree in my closet, but it's a small closet and Odell was bound to look inside of it and find his naked wife."

Attorney Elder nodded. "And I understand that Odell Crabtree first looked under your bed."

"That's right," Longarm said. "But his wife couldn't fit under it."

"Then what happened?" Attorney Elder asked.

"I kicked Odell in the ribs with my bare foot, hoping to subdue him, but he found his gun and I knew he was going to try and kill me. I shouted at him not to do it, and we both fired at the same moment. His shot was wide and shattered my window. My bullet was on target."

"So you fired in self-defense?"

"That's right," Longarm said. "Odell Crabtree would have fired a second shot at me, and the distance was so close that he would not have missed again. So I made my first shot count."

"Then what happened?"

"Etta came out of the closet and began to scream that I had murdered her husband."

"And she was naked and unharmed?"

"That's right. And that's when Etta told me that her husband was the only son of a rich man from Boston. She said that he'd hire the best lawyers in Boston and I'd hang for killing Odell, and that she would go back to Boston, take care of the old man and his wife before they died, and then inherit the Crabtree family fortune."

"Objection, your honor!"

"Objection overruled," Judge Henson snapped. "Go on with the testimony."

"There's not much left to say. At first I was pretty shocked at how calculating Etta was when she was talking about her rich in-laws. And I only half believed her. But when I questioned her about the Boston family, Etta asked me how I thought she and Odell had gotten to own the apartment building free and clear. I didn't know it was paid off, and she then admitted that Odell's 'old man' bought it for them and that she'd wind up a rich widow after Mr. Dunston Crabtree and his wife died. She said that she'd probably have to wipe shitty ass for a while, but she might be able to figure out a way to hasten the death of Mr. Dunston Crabtree and his ailing wife."

"Objection!" Lanier cried.

"Objection overruled," Judge Henson said. "And then what happened?"

"Etta had come into my apartment wearing a faded housedress. She tore her dress down from the neck and then raked her breasts with her own fingers. She said I'd go to the gallows and she'd start living like a queen in Boston after the senior Mr. Crabtree and his wife died."

Attorney Elder nodded. "So if Odell Crabtree had never woken up early from his Saturday night drunk and broken down the door, what do you suppose would have happened?"

Longarm looked at the jurors. "Etta would have come around the next Sunday, but I'd already decided that I didn't feel right about the arrangement, so I was going to look for a new apartment. I'd have found one and none of this would have happened to any of us."

"Do you have anything more to say?" Attorney Elder asked.

"Only that I made a huge mistake in letting the woman into my apartment and then making love to her. I knew right afterward that I had created a monster and I wanted out of the deal as quickly as possible. And when Odell Crabtree came into my apartment he was out of his mind with jealousy and rage. The truth is that I was weak of the flesh, and now I'm paying for that personal failing. But I'm an innocent man and I've earned the right to freedom after years of risking my life for the good of the public."

"Thank you," Attorney Elder said. "That is all that I have to ask my client, and now I will hand him over to the prosecution."

Attorney Lanier came out of his seat. "Marshal Long, how many men have you shot to death in your career?"

"I don't know."

"Hazard a guess."

Longarm knew this was a loaded question and that what he said next would shock both the judge and the jury. But he was under oath and there was no getting around a straight answer. "Maybe twenty."

"Maybe twenty? That's one hell of a lot of dead men. Does Odell Crabtree make twenty-one?"

"I don't know," Longarm snapped with exasperation. "I've never kept count. All I can say is that I've never killed a man that didn't either try to kill me first or deserved to die."

"Hmmm, I see," Lanier mused aloud. "So, no judge. No jury. Just *six-gun* justice. Is that your style, Marshal Long? Do you like to play judge, jury, and executioner all rolled into one?"

"Objection!" Attorney Elder cried. "The prosecution is trying to put words into my client's mouth."

"Objection sustained."

"All right then," Lanier said, "one more question and I'm through with Marshal Long. Do you often play the gigolo and take advantage of married women?"

"Objection!"

"Overruled. Answer the question, Marshal."

Longarm took a deep breath and chose his next words very carefully. "I can't tell you under oath that I've never made love to another man's wife. If I did so I would be lying. But I don't make a practice of it and I never pursue married women. Sometimes, though, it just happens. I like women and women seem to like me. I'm not ashamed of the fact and I've never tried to hide my affection for the opposite sex."

"Thank you," Attorney Lanier said, cutting Longarm off before he could continue. "No more questions."

"Then," Judge Henson said, "if there is no more testimony to be heard, I will ask the jury to convene and reach a verdict."

"One more witness," Attorney Lanier said. "And I'm sure Your Honor will agree that his testimony will be very valuable."

"And who would that be?"

"Our own Sheriff Bert Belcher."

"Objection," Attorney Elder cried, approaching the bench. "Your Honor, I can clearly establish that Sheriff Belcher has an intense dislike for my client and that his testimony would be biased if not completely false."

"I'm going to let the jury decide if that is true or not," the judge said after a moment's reflection.

"Sheriff Bert Belcher," Attorney Lanier called as the sheriff marched through the door into the courtroom to take his seat on the witness stand and be sworn in under oath.

"Sheriff Belcher, I understand that you have had Custis Long as your prisoner in your jail for almost three weeks. Is that correct?"

"It is."

"And has Custis Long been on good behavior?"

"He most certainly has not been! He's attacked no less than five of my other prisoners. He sent one to the hospital and seriously beat up the other four so bad that they could not walk and had to be attended to by a doctor."

"Liar!" Longarm shouted. "You've put five brawlers in my cell to either kill or maim me!"

"Silence!" the judge bellowed. "Custis Long, you are not on the witness stand anymore and you'd better keep your mouth shut or I'll have you gagged and removed from this courtroom!"

Longarm seethed and bit his lip to keep silent. It was clear now that Sheriff Belcher was the prosecution's ace in the hole and that he was going to put the nails in Longarm's coffin with his lying testimony.

"So, Sheriff, what else did you learn about the accused during his incarceration in your cell?"

"He admitted that he shot Odell Crabtree in cold blood and told me that he forcibly had his way with the man's wife."

"Like raping and sodomizing her?"

"Yeah. He said that he'd known Mrs. Crabtree was a former prostitute and so he figured she'd be used to rough stuff and that she'd even like it. When she didn't like it, he said it made him even more excited."

"Why did he tell you this if it could be used against him?"

"He was dead drunk in my cell. Someone had sneaked up in the alley behind the office and tossed him a bottle of whiskey through the bars. He'd drunk it all and was feeling crazy and wanted to brag. He swore me to secrecy, but I knew that I couldn't keep quiet, and so here I am."

"And this is your sworn oath?"

"So help me God," Bert Belcher said solemnly "I have never heard a more depraved account from a prisoner, and I've heard some terrible things in my time as lawman. He said one last thing that you might want to know."

Attorney Lanier feigned surprise. "And that is?"

The sheriff took a deep breath as though he was about to drag something out from deep in his soul. "Marshal Long told me that he raped, sodomized, and defiled Mrs. Crabtree because he wanted her to be afraid of him. So afraid that she would not resist marrying him."

"Marrying him?" Lanier asked as the audience and jurors gasped in shock.

"That's right. Marshal Long had it all figured out that he would force Mrs. Crabtree to marry him after he killed her husband, then he'd stand to get in line for the family's inheritance. He said he could charm the senior Crabtree and his wife, and then he'd be the one to make sure that their time left on earth would be short but not at all sweet."

"Did he actually brag and say how he was going to murder not only the son but also the father and mother?"

"Poison," Sheriff Belcher snapped. "Custis Long said he had seen a lot of it in his time and he knew exactly how he'd poison the rich old man and his old lady."

A murmur of outrage passed through the crowded courtroom, and then the judge cleared his throat and said, "I will now ask the jury to consider all the testimony and then reach a verdict. And I am quite sure that it will be justice served."

Longarm swallowed hard and tried to catch Sheriff Belcher's eye to let the man know that as long as he lived, he would try to exact revenge for the lies that had just been uttered.

But Sheriff Belcher left the witness stand with a tight smile on his fat face and wouldn't even look in Longarm's direction.

Chapter 11

Longarm sat with his head bowed in his cramped and dirty cell and waited for the bailiff to come and take him back to the courthouse, where he would face the decision of the jury. Given Sheriff Belcher's lying and damning testimony, Longarm had absolutely no doubt that he would be sentenced to hang. He'd been in plenty of courtrooms where men he'd arrested had been sentenced, and he knew by looking at the jurors' faces that he was as good as dead.

Damn Etta Crabtree and Officer Kunkle for their lies! But most of all, damn Sheriff Bert Belcher for dropping the noose over his head!

How long would he have left before he walked the gallows? Three days at least while they build even a flimsy scaffold. But more likely, they'd give him a week in this shit hole of a jail cell to fret and worry about his impending death. Even a week carrying the weight of a certain death sentence could break the will of most strong men.

Longarm was not afraid of dying, but he sure didn't want to die and leave a pack of liars to profit from his death. And he'd seen more than his share of men dance at the end of a hangman's noose, and it was not a pretty sight. It left a scarring and indelible memory on the mind. Yet, the public seemed to love watching the condemned man climb the scaffold and stand on the gallows with his head bowed and his eyes wild with terror, his entire body shaking as if he were old and had the palsy. They loved how a preacher would ask the condemned if he had any last words to say in order to cleanse his soul of guilt so that he would be received in Heaven.

A few condemned men would raise their heads and actually become defiant. They'd curse the preacher, the town, the people, and then laugh at the sky and the world in a final gesture to mock their awful, public death. But most men wept, or worse, sobbed and begged for their lives. Longarm had seen men on the gallows vacate their bowels and piss their pants while slobbering and wailing for mercy. Those were the worst, and he would be damned if he would beg, weep, or curse.

No, if he had to die, Longarm decided he would do it with his chin raised and his eyes fixed on his lying accusers. He would call their names and he would tell them that they were going to burn forever in hell. And then he would die a brave man and that would be his legacy.

"Mr. Long," a voice said, breaking through his dark reverie. "The jury has reached a verdict and the judge has asked me and these other men to escort you to the courtroom right now."

There were five large men, all heavily armed, standing in wait. Everyone knew what the verdict would be, and they weren't taking any chances should Longarm try to make a desperate escape.

"Turn around and put your hands behind your back,

Mr. Long, so I can handcuff you," the bailiff ordered. "Don't try any funny business. This ain't personal between you and me. This is just my job."

"I understand that," Longarm said, "and I do not hold any anger toward you. But you'd better understand that I am *still* a deputy United States marshal, and you'll address me that way."

"Yes, Marshal Long. Now, turn around and let me handcuff you so we can take the walk."

Longarm did as he was asked. There was no hope of escaping here and now . . . not with all these armed men watching his every move.

"All right, everyone, stand aside and let me take the prisoner to the courtroom," the bailiff said.

The armed men parted and one hissed, "You son-ofabitch! You're gonna get what you got comin'!"

Longarm bit back a reply, and with guns pointed at his back, he walked out of the cell, out of the sheriff's office, across the street, and through the courthouse doors.

The tension in Hanging Judge Henson's courtroom was at the point of breaking. Longarm avoided the eyes of everyone as he was led to his chair and told to sit.

"All rise for the judge," the bailiff called.

Everyone stood and then sat as Judge Henson, with his cup full of tequila sloshing on the floor, tottered into his chair. "Has the jury reached a unanimous decision?"

"It has," the lead juror said.

"Then read it out loud."

The man cleared his throat nervously and said in a voice that was strained and high pitched, "We find the accused, Custis Long, *guilty* of murder in the first degree."

The courtroom erupted in a buzz and there was a cheer and then loud applause. The judge gaveled everyone to silence and then asked, "And now it is my duty to pronounce an appropriate sentence. And that sentence is that former Marshal Custis Long be sentenced to hang by the neck until dead, and that such sentence shall be carried out this next Saturday in a public place."

Attorney Elder shook his head, leaned in close to Longarm, and said, "I'm so very sorry I failed you."

"You didn't fail me," Longarm told him. "After the way that Etta and the sheriff perjured themselves, no one could have gotten me justice."

"I know, but . . ."

"Let go of it, Carson," Longarm ordered in a voice that did not sound like his own. "You did your very best and I'm satisfied with that. You should be satisfied as well."

Judge Henry Henson gaveled his courtroom into silence once more, then looked at Longarm and said, "Do you have anything to say?"

Longarm came to his feet, turned, and addressed not the jury but the audience. "I killed Odell Crabtree in self-defense, and I made love to his wife because I was weak, feeling broke, and was generally stupid. But I don't deserve to be found guilty of murder, and in the end, the truth will be revealed and *real justice* will be served."

"Bailiff," the judge called, "escort the prisoner back to his cell and tell the carpenters that I want them to work night and day if necessary to see that a proper and impressive gallows is built in the town square. We're going to have one helluva big crowd for this hanging, and I want a first-class job to be done all around."

"Yes, Your Honor!"

Longarm was grabbed by both arms and hustled down the aisle toward the door. As he passed Billy Vail, his boss whispered, "I swear I'll find a way."

Longarm nodded and then he saw Dunston P. Crabtree and his manservant, Reinhold, step into the aisle to block their progression out of the courthouse.

"You gentlemen will have to sit back down and let us pass," the bailiff ordered.

But the two men stood immovable. Then the elder Crabtree looked Longarm straight in the eyes and asked, "Do you swear on the soul of your mother and father that you have told the court the truth?"

"I do. And furthermore, you knew your son was flawed and you know what kind of a woman he married," Longarm said. "If I were you, Mr. Crabtree, I'd watch out for myself and my wife. You've got a viper in the Crabtree family, and that viper is about to slither her way into Boston."

Dunston Crabtree blinked and then he and his bodyguard let them pass.

Chapter 12

Sheriff Belcher had moved Longarm to another cell, one in which the barred window looked out toward the square so that his prisoner could watch the gallows construction.

"Yes, sir!" Belcher chortled. "I got seven carpenters all workin' on that gallows, and it'll be the best that was ever built . . . at least in Denver."

"Glad to hear that," Longarm said as he lay on his bunk with his hands folded behind his head for a pillow.

"And I got my favorite hangman comin' all the way from Pueblo. When he heard it was you that was going to swing, he begged to be the one who would put the noose around your neck."

"Ah," Longarm said, refusing to be upset by a man that he loathed. "That would be old Ike Reedy."

"Yes, sir! He's the one, all right. Ike Reedy swears that he's hanged more than fifty men, and I wouldn't doubt it one little bit. He says that he ties a knot in his rope that is sure to break a man's neck when he falls through the trap . . . most of the time. Of course, as we all know, if your neck don't get broke, you just kick and strangle until the life is choked out of you."

Longarm looked over at Belcher and said, "You know what?"

"What?"

"You're one sick and sadistic sonofabitch, Belcher. And I'll tell you something else. I'm not going to hang, and I'm coming for you. And when I get my hands on you, I'll strangle *you* to death."

Belcher's smile slipped. "Well, that's mighty free talk for a man who is going to swing in two days. And you know what they always say."

"What's that?"

"Talk is cheap," the sheriff said. "I've watched a lot of men hang, but you'll be the prize. Yes, sir, Ike Reedy sent me a telegram from Pueblo askin' me how much you weigh, and you know what I told him?"

"Don't know and don't care," Longarm replied.

"I told him that you weighed about one hundred and sixty pounds."

"You know that even after being in this shit hole I still weigh over two hundred. So why did you lie to Ike?"

The sheriff began to laugh. "Well, I'm hoping that when you drop the knot *doesn't* break your neck and we get to see you dance all your way into hell!"

"Retribution," Longarm said, turning his eyes to the ceiling. "That's what's coming your way, Belcher. But the thing of it is that you're just too mean and dumb to know it."

"I may be mean and dumb, but three nights from now I'll be gettin' drunk and howlin' at the moon while I piss on your fresh grave!"

Longarm closed his eyes and tried to sleep.

* * *

After being searched from head to toe, Billy Vail came early the second day and brought Longarm a big breakfast plate of ham, eggs, and flapjacks. "This ought to raise your spirits a mite."

Longarm shook his head. "I'm not very hungry, Billy. But I do appreciate your concern."

"You're going to need your strength when we break you out of here."

"And how do you propose to do that?"

Billy shrugged. "I'm going to just walk in here tonight, pull a gun on the guards, make them give me the keys, and we'll waltz out of here together."

"No," Longarm said in a hard, flat voice. "You've got a fine wife and children, and I'm not about to let you ruin your life that way."

"Well, what else can I do?" Billy leaned up against the bars and his voice had a tremor. "I'm just not going to let you hang, Custis. I know you're a fool when it comes to women, and this time that foolishness really got you in a bad, bad fix. But you're not going to hang because of two lying witnesses."

"Let me think about this," Longarm said. "I'm working on an idea or two. The thing is that I don't want to have to kill any of the sheriff's men. If it wasn't for that, I'd be pretty confident of escaping."

"Your attorney, Carson Elder, went to the judge and asked him for a retrial, saying that if he had more time he could have come up with a better defense."

"I appreciate that," Longarm said. "But the judge said no."

"That's right," Billy admitted. "Judge Henson just laughed out loud in Attorney Elder's face. He said that if you had a whole year you wouldn't come up with any fresh evidence that would prove your innocence."

"The judge is right."

"I'm so desperate that I've even had a couple of our men out in the alley looking for the bullet that Odell fired at you . . . but no luck."

"You'll never find it, and even if you did, you couldn't link it to what happened. That's a waste of time, Billy."

"But I can't just . . . just do nothing!"

"I'm working on a plan," Longarm told his friend and boss. "Don't lose hope."

Billy lowered his voice. "Can you tell me a little of it?"

"Nope."

The truth of it was that Longarm hadn't been able to come up with any good plan short of killing the sheriff's men and escaping. And maybe on the last night he'd even be willing to do that . . . but he doubted it.

"The sheriff isn't letting me come but once a day, so I'll be back tomorrow morning. I'm going to leave the plate so you can eat after I'm gone . . . if you change your mind."

"Thanks again, and thank your wife."

"She's really, really upset about all this. We consider you family, Custis."

Longarm felt a knot form in his throat, and it was all he could do to nod his head in understanding and then turn and go back to his bunk to stare at the ceiling.

"You've got another visitor," the sheriff announced that evening. "But I sure as hell don't know what he's here for."

"Who's that?"

"Me," Dunston Crabtree said, turning to his manservant. "Reinhold, I'll be fine in here. Just wait."

The man nodded and Longarm caught his eye for a

moment. Reinhold's eyes were pale green like those of a cat that Longarm had once kept in his apartment.

"I sure don't understand this," the sheriff complained. "But I guess you just want to look the killer of your son in the eye and tell him what a murderin' bastard he is and how much you'll enjoy watching him swing, huh, Mr. Crabtree?"

The old man nodded. "Now, go back to your desk and leave us alone for a few minutes, Sheriff."

Belcher was being dismissed like a child and he didn't like it, but he managed to nod his head and leave.

Longarm sat up and looked across his cell at the old man. "What *are* you here for?"

"I took my daughter-in-law to the nicest restaurant in Denver last night."

"And that would be?"

"The Paladin."

"Yeah," Longarm said. "That's one of my favorites, although I rarely can afford to eat there."

"How much money do you make as a federal officer?" Crabtree asked.

"Less than fifty a month."

"Fifty a month is nothing," Dunston Crabtree said. "I spent that much last night on lobster and steaks for Etta and myself . . . and Reinhold, of course. But then we were drinking expensive French wine by the bottle."

"That's real nice," Longarm said, not having a clue as to where this conversation would lead.

"Etta drank way too much and got drunk."

"Is that right."

"I knew she would," the old man said. "And then I had Reinhold escort her back to her apartment building and pretend that he wanted to go to bed with the slut."

"I see."

"No," Dunston Crabtree told him. "You don't see at all. How could you be so stupid as to make that kind of rent arrangement with Etta?"

"I dunno," Longarm confessed. "It was one of those days when I guess I woke up on the wrong side of the bed. I looked in the mirror and saw a lawman that was living from payday to payday with not a cent saved and the prospect of getting old staring him hard in the face."

"I'll bet your parents had high hopes for you, huh?"

"Yeah," Longarm said. "I come from West Virginia and my father was almost as successful as you . . . until the war."

"What did he want you to be?"

Longarm rubbed the sockets of his eyes with the palms of his hands and shook his head in discouragement. "Why are you asking me these questions, Mr. Crabtree?"

"I'd like to know about the man who shot my son to death."

"I'm not going to give you the satisfaction."

"I didn't think you would," Crabtree replied.

"You want to tell me that you're going out to the Paladin tonight and have another great supper . . . or what?"

"I don't need to do that now," Crabtree said quietly. "I found out what I really needed to know from Etta last night. And what she didn't blab to us at the table as she drank glass after glass of expensive wine, she told Reinhold in her bed."

Longarm wasn't tracking this even a little. "Mr. Crabtree, why don't you just get to the point and quit beating around the bush."

"All right then, I will." The wealthy old man leaned in close to the bars and used a forefinger to beckon Longarm to his side. "What I learned is what I suspected after hearing you and Etta give testimony."

"And that is?"

"You were telling the truth; Etta was lying just as she always has."

"And Reinhold confirmed that in Etta's bedroom?"

"That's right. He took a few bottles of champagne with him to her apartment and she became so drunk that she told him the truth about how she had made that rent arrangement with you and that my son had burst into your apartment with a gun and fired first. Etta laughed and laughed about how she, Officer Kunkle, and Sheriff Belcher had all gotten together and worked out their testimonies. Testimonies that were false and were guaranteed to get you sent to the gallows."

"I'll be damned." Longarm shook his head. "But even if you went to the judge he'd say that it would be your word against Etta's. And you know that Etta will sober up and say that she never confessed to anything. She'll swear that on the Bible knowing that if she didn't, Sheriff Belcher would kill her or have her killed."

"I'm sure that is true," Crabtree said. "But, while she was trying to get undressed, she actually asked Reinhold to help her murder me and my wife so that she could get the inheritance. She offered Reinhold thirty percent of whatever is in my estate."

"And he had to hump Etta to get that out of her?"

Dunston Crabtree looked offended. "Reinhold would kill for me if I asked, but I'd never ask and I most certainly wouldn't ask him to copulate with that lying slut of a daughter-in-law! No, Reinhold just kept pouring the champagne until Etta passed out cold."

Longarm bowed his head a moment in thought. Then he lifted his chin and looked the old man in the eye through the cell bars. "So now that you really know the truth, what are you going to do about it? You can't get

Hanging Judge Henson to change his mind, and there isn't time to get some higher authority to demand a stay of execution."

"Yes, so your attorney told me," Crabtree admitted. "So that only leaves one option."

"Me hanging?"

"No. You made a terrible mistake, but you didn't murder my son. Odell was bad to the bone. I kicked him out of my house when he was eighteen because he was screwing the maids and beating up on all my servants. He stole the silver and sold it, and he was trying to figure out a way to get into my bank accounts when I sent him packing."

"Etta claims that you bought her and Odell that apartment building."

"I did. It seemed like a cheap price to give Odell and that witch of a wife of his a place to anchor here in Denver and stay away from my wife and me in Boston. And for quite a few years, it worked. But when you shot Odell in self-defense, that changed everything, and now Etta wants to come live with my wife and myself at our mansion. That, of course, will never happen, nor will she inherit a dime of my fortune."

"What will you do with it?"

"My dear wife and I have founded a number of charities around Boston. Homeless children . . . sick and abandoned dogs . . . the hospitals. Those sorts of organizations that do make things better and considerably ease the suffering of humans and animals that cannot take care of themselves through no fault of their own."

"That's great," Longarm told the old man with sincerity. "So you're leaving your entire fortune to these charities and charitable foundations?"

"Yes, except for a bit of money for Reinhold, who has

served me with loyalty, discretion, and competence since I hired him as a lad many years ago. You see, Reinhold has become for my wife and me the son we never had but wished we'd had."

"I understand. But what is all of this . . ."

"To do with you, Marshal Custis Long?"

"Frankly, yes."

"I'm going to have Reinhold break you out of here tonight and then help you get out of Denver. He will travel with you wherever you choose to run and hide while I will remain here in Denver, twisting arms and figuring out a way to clear your good name."

"Whoa!" Longarm whispered. "Before we get into restoring my reputation, how is your man Reinhold going to spring me from this jail? There are at least three heavily armed deputies here twenty-four hours a day, and they aren't stupid or slow."

"Exactly how Reinhold gets you out of here hasn't been decided yet, but I assure you that he will do it. Whenever I ask Reinhold to do something, it is as good as done. Reinhold has studied the martial arts in Japan and has made it his mission in life to prepare himself for any kind of trouble that might pass my way from the many enemies I've made while building my fortune."

"I wish I shared your confidence in Reinhold," Longarm said, trying not to get his hopes too high.

"It *will* be done. I asked Reinhold to stay with you for a month while I clear your name of all the charges."

"Do you really think that is possible?"

"Of course, it is."

"Judge Henson will never allow . . ."

Dunston Crabtree waved his old hand as if swatting away a fly. "He can be convinced of the error of his sentence . . . one way or another."

"You're going to *buy* him?"

"I didn't say that. Sometimes there are better, more convincing things that you can offer a man than money."

Longarm frowned. "What . . ."

"Don't ask," Crabtree warned. "Just be ready tonight when Reinhold comes for you, and start thinking about where you want to go."

Longarm was silent for a long time, and then he said, "If this really happens, I will be in your debt forever, Mr. Crabtree."

"No, you won't. You warned me about Etta, and that warning led me to the action that was taken last night and will be taken when you are on the run."

"Reinhold would be better off staying here with you," Longarm said. "I don't need any companionship or help."

"Maybe yes and maybe no, but that's the way it will be if you want *my* help."

"In that case, I accept."

"I wish that you had been my son . . . then Reinhold would have had a brother at least close to his equal."

"I had a good childhood and good parents," Longarm told the wealthy old man. "I would not dishonor them by saying I wish I had been raised by another couple and in a different manner and place."

"I respect that from you," Crabtree said, squeezing Longarm's shoulder through the bars. "Now, I've asked Reinhold not to kill any of the officers when he comes tonight. If that happened, then nothing I could do or say would save you from an eventual noose, and I certainly don't want to lose Reinhold."

"I understand. What you are saying is that I can't kill anyone if things go amiss tonight."

"Exactly so."

"Sir, you have my word that will not happen."

"Then I am satisfied and there is nothing left to say between us," Crabtree told him.

"Will I see you again before I leave Denver with Reinhold?"

"No."

"Then thank you very much, Mr. Crabtree. You are a remarkable man."

"And I'm told that you are the same. Good night and good luck!"

Chapter 13

By sunset, when the last carpenter had driven the last nail into the almost finished gallows, Longarm realized that this had been the longest day of his life. Now he sat waiting in his cell while Sheriff Belcher and a pack of his officers shared a few bottles of whiskey out in the front office. The sheriff and his men were celebrating because tomorrow was Saturday and the big event: Longarm's hanging. The carpenters had all been ordered to return to work at daybreak in order to have the gallows finished and tested by noon. The hanging itself was going to take place at one o'clock, and by then half the men in Denver would be in the saloons getting drunk in anticipation of the widely publicized and highly anticipated event.

Sheriff Belcher had crowed to Longarm that wagonloads of miners were coming in from distant gold and silver mining towns like Central City and Leadville. Their town's best prostitutes were coming along too, for they understood that this weekend would be their bonanza. And to top it all off, a special "hanging party" train was coming up from Pueblo and it was sold out, as was the train coming south from Cheyenne with standing-room-only crowds.

Public hangings were always widely heralded and attended, and the atmosphere in most towns before a necktie party was almost the equal of Fourth of July celebrations. Longarm had no idea why a hanging attracted so many excited curiosity seekers, but it always did. Denver had held many hangings, and sometimes Judge Henson made it possible for three or four men to be hanged at the same time.

It was great for business, and it made people forget their own problems.

"Well," Belcher said, opening the door between the front office and the line of dark and dingy cells in the back, "I'm going home to get some sleep. Tomorrow is going to be a big day here in Denver. The city fathers and Chamber of Commerce are sure pleased about all the out-of-towners coming in to drink and spend money."

"I'm glad that I'm such a boon for the local economy," Longarm replied sarcastically.

Belcher rubbed his hands in glee.

"The hangman, Ike Reedy, is out there in front with my boys showing off the rope that he's going to use to make you dance on air. Oh, and it's a fine, new rope! Ike has even oiled it. And you've never in your life seen such a big knot! Yep, Ike says that he'll put it just behind your right ear and that, if we get lucky and the crowd isn't too noisy, we'll be able to hear your neck crack sounding like a dry tree limb."

"It's always nice to meet a man who enjoys his work," Longarm said. "And I'm happy to help out the local merchants and businessmen."

"Oh," Belcher said, playing along, "we all knew you would be. Did you know that Hanging Judge Henson is half-owner of both the Blue Dog Saloon and Cody Hotel?"

Longarm shrugged. "No, I can't say that I did. The Cody Hotel is one of the biggest and best in Denver."

"Three stories and forty-seven rooms. And guess who owns the other half of it?"

"You do?"

"That's right," Belcher said, rubbing his hands together. "You see, the judge and I go back a ways, and he understands that we have a good thing going in this town together. I know that he is a thief who has taken money to influence his sentencing, and he knows that I have a profitable business giving some of the businesses in this town *special favors* and protection."

"Is that a fact," Longarm said. "Bert, I'd always suspected that you were extorting money from some of the businesses."

"'Extorting' is kind of an ugly word. What I do and what some of my people help me do is to just give those businesses that want things to go smoothly a little *special* protection."

"You're even slimier that I thought you were, although what you're telling me about the judge isn't all that surprising," Longarm said.

"I don't give a damn what you say or think about me," Belcher said. "But I did want to thank you for all the extra money that you're going to be putting in our pockets. Why, tonight Judge Henson confided in me that these hangings always mean that his businesses do a huge increase in business. The judge was in high spirits and reckoned your hanging will fatten his wallet by at least two thousand dollars this weekend."

"How about that," Longarm said. "So the judge has a serious monetary interest in sentencing men to hang."

"Oh, yeah! He profits greatly from hangings. That's why he's ordered so many in his time."

"I'll remember that," Longarm said. "And I'll remember that right after I settle my debt with you, I'll settle it with our corrupt hanging judge."

"Ha!" Belcher laughed. "My, but you should listen to yourself, Custis! Here you are in my jail with less than twenty-four hours to live, and you're threatening me and the judge? My gawd, you must be delusional or else you just can't face the fact that you're not going to be around by this time tomorrow."

Belcher hooked his thumbs into his gun belt and leaned back against the wall with a smile on his fat face. "At this time tomorrow you'll be lying on a slab in the mortician's office and he'll probably be charging fifty cents a head just for people to pass by and take a peek at your purple face and bulging eyes."

"Between now and then," Longarm said, "maybe I'll tell a few of my last-minute visitors what you've just told me, because you've obviously had too much to drink and aren't thinking too clearly this evening."

"I'm drunk, but not stupid drunk," Belcher said. "Custis, the fact is that you're not going to have any 'last-minute visitors.' Not tonight and not tomorrow morning. Not even on your walk to the gallows, because I'm going to have you handcuffed wrist and ankle and *gagged* before we leave this jail for your last walk."

Longarm took a deep breath and pointed a forefinger at the sheriff. "I hope you're the one who comes into this cell and tries to gag me, Sheriff. I sure do hope that you're man enough to try that."

Belcher chuckled. "Like I said, I'm not stupid, and I won't be drunk tomorrow morning or do anything dumb. You'll have no teary-eyed last-minute visitors. No favorite last meal. No last-minute appeal from some out-of-town judge granting a stay of execution. In short, no one will be able to see or speak to you between now and when you drop through the trapdoor. How's that suit your fancy, huh?"

Belcher's smile died and his voice got mean. "Custis, I've watched a lot of men hang, but you're going to be my all-time favorite. And I promise you, I will piss on your fresh grave. Why, I might even drop my pants and shit on it too!"

Longarm had heard all the bile he could stand for one evening. "Your day is coming, Belcher. And when it does, it won't be pretty."

"You just scare the hell out of me," the sheriff answered. "I'm so scared that I'm going home to sleep like a baby. I wonder if you'll be able to sleep on your last night? Huh?"

Longarm had a full chamber pot under his bunk, and when the sheriff began to laugh, Longarm scooped it up in one swift motion and hurled it at the braying bastard. The chamber pot shattered on his cell bars and a spray of shit and piss covered Belcher from head to toe.

The big sheriff howled in fury and rage. Belcher yanked his gun out of his holster and cried, "You dirty, dead sonofabitch. I'm going to shoot you full of holes!"

"If you do it," Longarm said, smiling, "the whole town will either tar and feather you or hang you in my place so they still have someone to watch dance on a rope tomorrow. So go ahead and see how popular you become when I'm dead in this cell of gunshot wounds."

Belcher was quaking. Shit and piss covered his hair and dripped down his face. The front of his shirt was heavily splattered, as were his pants and even his boots.

Longarm chuckled. "You look exactly like a fountain of shit, so why don't you spit my piss out of your mouth and complete the image?"

Belcher raised his gun and took aim. His hand shook and he had to wipe urine and feces from his face in order to see. And right then, Longarm realized he just might have pushed the sick sonofabitch just a little bit too far.

"Sheriff!" a voice said. "Don't!"

It was Officer Kunkle and he was grabbing Belcher by the arm and spinning him around. "My gawd," he cried, recoiling from the stench and the sight of his boss. "What happened?"

"Take a guess, asshole!"

Kunkle peeked around the door into the cells and saw the shattered chamber pot. "Oh my gawd," he whispered. "Marshal Long really got you back."

"Shut up, you sorry excuse for a lawman! Damn you, Kunkle, get in there and get that mess cleaned up!"

There was a long pause. "Yes, sir."

Longarm listened as Sheriff Belcher shouted and raised hell out in the office among his officers before the front door slammed. Only then was Longarm sure that the sheriff was gone for the night.

"You really did it to him," Kunkle said with a hint of admiration in his voice.

"He got what he deserved."

Kunkle left for a few minutes, then returned with a mop and bucket of fresh water. "Marshal Long, I can't believe that the sheriff didn't shoot you right where you stand."

"Oh," Longarm said, "he sure wanted to. But I

reminded him that if he did he would be the most un-popular man in Denver. I mean, think about it, Kunkle. All those hundreds and maybe even thousands of specta-tors coming from far and wide just to see me do the rope dance. I told Belcher that he might just have to take my place or he'd be tarred and feathered for ruining such a great event."

Kunkle began to mop the floor.

"How come you're doing this and not one of the of-ficers out in the front office that you outrank?"

"I don't 'outrank' anyone here," Kunkle confessed. "I'm low dog on the totem pole. I get all the shit jobs."

"I take it that you are not Sheriff Belcher's favorite officer."

"You can say that again."

"And yet, you lied on the witness stand for him and Etta Crabtree so that I'd hang."

Kunkle stopped mopping and stared at the stone floor for a long time before he lowered his voice to a whisper. "Marshal Long, I'm not going to get this chance again to speak while we're alone, so I'm just going to say what I need to say right now. The truth is that I'm sorry I lied on the witness stand. I'll carry the burden of guilt to my grave over what I had to do."

"'Had to do'?" Longarm asked.

"Sure. I wanted to quit this job and try to find another after what happened to Odell Crabtree and all the stuff afterward, but the sheriff made me stay on and then falsely testify at your trial. If I refused, he said that he'd not only see that I didn't live . . . but he'd have my fam-ily killed too. I got a wife and two kids. What else could I do?"

"You could have packed up in the night and run off with your family."

"They'd have come after me. I'd never have gotten away alive with my family. And I've got a lot of bills. My wife had trouble with delivering our second child. We're deep in debt and I need this job just to keep a roof over my head and feed the wife and kids."

Longarm expelled a deep breath. "And so, to do that you are going to let an *innocent* man hang?"

Kunkle shook his head in misery. "Marshal Long, I'm really, really sorry."

"Sorry isn't good enough," Longarm told him in a hard voice. Then, softening his voice, he asked, "Listen, Kunkle, if you left this job what would you do?"

"I got a brother in Gold Hill, Nevada. It's on the Comstock Lode someplace."

"I've been there."

"Is it nice?"

"It's a hard-rock mining town on the side of Sun Mountain. Not much water. Not many trees and a lot of wind and heat in the summer but it's a boomtown and there are good people trying to make their living in the deep, company-owned mines."

"My brother has a newspaper that is really doing well. When we were kids we always said we'd go into the newspaper business together. John said if I could come out there and bring just three hundred dollars, then he'd sell me half the business."

"And that's what you'd like to do?"

"More than anything in the world. John says that working together we could even buy a press down in Carson City, which is the territorial capital of Nevada, and that we'd do really well. That's why I need three hundred dollars. But I can't even pay my current bills, let alone pay the fare to get my family moved and come up with that kind of money."

Longarm chose his next words carefully. "Kunkle, what if I or someone else gave you the money to tell the truth about what really happened that Sunday morning at my apartment? What could you honestly say to prove that I shot Odell Crabtree in self-defense?"

"I'd say that I saw a gun in Odell Crabtree's fist as he was lying there on your floor, and when I turned away Etta Crabtree took the gun and hid it."

"You'd say that?"

"What does it matter what I'd say?" Kunkle replied, furiously beginning to mop the floor. "I just need to get this dirty job done and go home. I . . . I just need to get away and never come back."

"Talk to Mr. Dunston Crabtree when I'm gone," Longarm hissed. "Tell him *exactly* what you just told me."

"And get myself and Mr. Crabtree probably killed by the sheriff or one of his men?" Kunkle tried to laugh. "No, thanks!"

"Do it," Longarm urged. "It could be the key to everything you want to do with your life."

Kunkle slammed his mop into the bucket with frustration. "Let's stop talking! I'm going to get this job finished and leave and . . . and I am sorry about what I did to you."

"I know that you are, and thanks for telling me the truth," Longarm said quietly. "And it would be a good idea if you left this place just as soon as you can tonight."

"I will, believe me. They're all laughing and getting drunk and I think it's disgusting to celebrate your hanging and . . . Oh, never mind!"

Kunkle finished the mopping and looked to be almost in tears as he hurried out of sight.

Longarm gave the man some thought. Earlier, Officer

Kunkle had been the number three man on his list to get even with for putting him on a straight path to the gallows. Now, Longarm decided that he would not come after Kunkle for revenge, and maybe the tormented would-be newspaperman might somehow even be the key to Longarm's desperate quest for justice and redemption.

Chapter 14

That Friday night Denver was packed with people who had come from the mountains and the plains in order to see a famous former United States marshal walk the gallows and then do his death dance. The hotels were filled and the saloons were doing a landmark business. Liquor flowed like water and the prostitutes had men lined up at their doors.

In the sheriff's office, five heavily armed deputies were playing penny-ante poker and sipping whiskey as they listened to the celebrations going on out in the streets and saloons. The room where they played was dense with cigar and cigarette smoke and the leftovers from a meal brought to the office by a Chinese cook.

"Gonna be a long night," one of the lawmen said with a yawn. "Sure wish I was out there with the rest of the folks havin' a high old time. Sounds like they're really on a tear."

"Yeah," another officer said. "There's bound to be some fights and trouble, and we should go out and keep a lid on things."

"We ain't supposed to do that. The sheriff said we were to stay inside and keep a watch on Custis Long. We don't open the front door for anybody, and we don't go out even if there's a damned shooting on the street."

"Does Belcher really think that anyone would try to storm this office and free Custis Long?"

"Hell, I don't know. But orders are orders. We're supposed to take a peek into the back to make sure that he stays put in his cell and that he ain't misbehaving."

"What the hell for?" another officer growled. "Is the sheriff worried that Custis Long is going to sprout wings and fly through the barred window? He's as good as hanged, and it's pretty dumb that the five of us have to spend the whole night sitting here in this office."

"Orders are orders, Joe. We just do as we're told tonight. You know that Belcher is as nervous as a flea on a hot skillet about Custis Long finding a way to escape."

"Ain't gonna happen."

Officer Dermit Kunkle listened to all this without comment or interest. He knew full well that Sheriff Belcher was going to fire him just as soon as Custis Long was hanged. Kunkle couldn't get his mind past his earlier conversation with the condemned United States marshal and he felt a deep sense of guilt and betrayal for the false testimony that he'd been forced to offer in the courtroom. And even after admitting that to Custis Long, the condemned man had not cursed nor did he seem to hate him. Kunkle wished more than anything in the world that he could just leave Denver and go to Nevada. He couldn't bear the idea of watching an innocent man hang and he'd probably be the only person in Denver who wasn't going to enjoy the necktie party tomorrow.

"Hey, Kunkle!"

"Yeah."

"What did you and that marshal have to talk about?"

"Oh, nothing much. I just asked him if he were afraid to die."

"I'll bet he said that he wasn't, and I can tell you right now that was a damn lie. Ain't never been a man that faced the noose that wasn't scared out of his mind. We all have bets on whether Custis Long will break before they drop the trapdoor. I say that he will shit his pants and piss 'em too! You want in on the bet?"

Dermit Kunkle swallowed hard. "No, thanks."

"Come on and get in on the action. I got a feeling you think that Custis Long is one hell of a man. Why don't you put some money down on whether he cracks or not?"

Kunkle didn't have much money, but he didn't like being shown up and made to look weak or foolish. "What are the odds that he won't break and empty himself or break down and beg?"

"Ten to one says he'll break down and cry or piss and shit in his pants before he drops."

Kunkle pulled out three dollars. "I'll take those odds. I'll lay money down that Custis Long will walk the gallows and drop without a tremble in his voice or a falter to his gait. He'll look out at the crowd and I'll bet he'll even smile."

"Smile!" one of the officers crowed. "Well, isn't he your idol? You must really admire Custis Long, huh?"

"I sure as shootin' do," Kunkle told the men at the table. And then he recklessly added, "He's a better man than I am, and he's a better man than anyone in this office."

The lawmen playing poker had been grinning at Kunkle, having their fun with a man that they knew would not be among them in a few days and would be walking the streets looking for work . . . any kind of work. But after Kunkle's words, their smiles were replaced by sneers and expressions of disgust.

"Kunkle, it's like Sheriff Belcher says. You're the saddest excuse anyone has ever seen for a law officer. You really aren't man enough to wear the pants in your own family, much less a badge."

Officer Kunkle was not a very large or strong young man, and he had been bullied almost all of his life. He'd taken whippings from bigger kids and from bigger men so often he couldn't remember how many times his nose had been broken and his lips split open. But through all the beatings he'd never backed down, never begged, and never crawled. And from all the beatings he'd suffered he had learned quite a few things about fighting. Namely, how to end a fight against a bigger man in a hurry.

"Did you hear me, Dermit? I say you're not much of a man."

"Fuck you, Hank," Kunkle snapped.

Officer Hank Colby was one of the bigger and tougher officers that worked for Belcher, and he was the sheriff's clear-cut favorite. Colby, already about half drunk and angry because he'd already lost two dollars in what was going to be an all-night poker vigil, erupted out of his chair.

"I'm gonna kick your sorry ass, Kunkle! Kick it right out the door."

"I'm not going anywhere," Kunkle said, raising his fists. "So come on and get me, big man."

"Hey!" the officer named Joe shouted. "If you guys bust up the office in here, Sheriff Belcher is going to come down on top of all of us. So take it outside and into the street."

Colby grabbed his whiskey bottle and threw down a

couple of slugs. "This is going to be fun," he said, grinning at his friends.

"But we ain't supposed to unlock that door," one of the officers said. "Those were Belcher's orders. Remember?"

"This won't take but a minute," Colby promised.

The front door of the office was then unlocked and Kunkle marched outside with his heart hammering in his chest. He stepped over the boardwalk and into the dirt street, turned, and took a few deep breaths as he worked out a plan that might give him a chance to win this lopsided fight.

Officer Hank Colby charged out the door and came at the smaller officer with his big fists flying. Kunkle stood his ground, and when Colby was almost on top of him, he kicked the big man right between the legs.

Colby's mouth flew open as he bent over and grabbed at his crotch. Kunkle kicked him in the face, his boot catching Colby under the chin and straightening him up again.

One more fast kick to the side of Colby's knee sent the big deputy sprawling in the dirt and a crowd of drunken celebrants came rushing over to watch the fight.

"Get up, Hank!" Dermit Kunkle was dancing on his toes. "Get up and take it like a man."

Hank Colby couldn't believe that he was in so much pain. His balls felt as if they had been blasted by a shotgun and the pain was excruciating. His knee wasn't working properly and his vision was blurred from the vicious kick to his chin. But he was aware the entire sheriff's office was standing out on the porch, gaping with disbelief, and that there was a crowd rapidly gathering around them in the street, shouting for him to make a good fight of it.

Colby cursed in anger and surged to his feet, one leg

feeling stiff and wooden. "You little pissant! Come here and fight!"

Dermit Kunkle's blood was up and he knew that he had hurt his opponent. He also knew that, if Hank Colby got a hand on him and threw him to the ground, the bigger and heavier man would overpower him and the fight would turn against him in an instant.

"Come on!" Colby yelled. "Get up here and fight me toe-to-toe!"

Dermit Kunkle tossed caution aside and danced forward. He weighed 145 pounds soaking wet and Colby had at least a sixty-pound advantage, but the man was slow and he was hurt.

Kunkle jabbed a slender arm out and his bony fist connected solidly with Colby's nose. Blood spurted and Colby surged forward, wrapping his arms about Kunkle in a powerful bear hug as he hissed, "You little bastard, now I'm going to break your backbone in half!"

Kunkle was trapped. Colby began to slam his heavy forehead into Kunkle's face. Bright lights danced behind Dermit Kunkle's eyes and he felt Colby's thick and powerful arms slide down to the base of his spine as the pressure intensified.

Suddenly, Kunkle felt the pressure go away! Hank Colby was being lifted from him as if he had been jerked skyward with a rope.

Kunkle staggered up against a hitching post and shook his head as he saw the man named Reinhold kick and chop and punch Hank Colby fast and hard. The deputy kept backpedaling until he tripped over the boardwalk, got up for a second, and then took more blows to windmill backward through the big front window of Livingston's Hardware Store.

All the deputies had watched in astonished silence

when Officer Kunkle had taken an early and surprising advantage over Hank Colby. But when Colby had finally wrapped the much smaller man up in his massive arms, they'd cheered knowing the fight was as good as finished. Now, this man from Boston had jumped into the fight uninvited and he was tearing their friend and fellow officer a new asshole, and that just would not do.

So the officers attacked Reinhold as a single body and the crowd cheered as the Boston man began to fight like a demon. Some of the spectators who were more liquored up than others got so excited that they began to throw their own kicks and punches, and in seconds there was a huge melee going on right out in front of the sheriff's office. And it was one hell of a lot of fun.

Officer Kunkle staggered toward the sheriff's office, his back feeling broken and his face bloodied from the pounding it had taken from Colby's brutal head butting. He entered the office and was about to collapse in a chair and cradle his head when he saw the jail cell keys lying right before his eyes on Sheriff Belcher's paper-littered desk.

Dermit Kunkle's hand reached out and he clutched the keys, then he stood up with blood trickling down his face. He knew that a full-scale riot was underway outside and he didn't understand any of it. He only knew that this was his one chance . . . the single, life-defining moment when he could forever erase the guilt that would destroy him as surely as a cancer.

Kunkle snatched up the keys, raced through the back door, and unlocked Longarm's cell.

"What the hell happened to you!" Longarm asked, pushing out of his cell.

"Doesn't matter. Just go! Run for your life!"

Longarm hurried past the bloodied Kunkle and charged

into the front office. He saw a rifle case and selected a double-barreled shotgun. He made sure it was loaded and also took a pistol from someone's desk and jammed it behind his waistband.

Longarm started to exit the office but he paused and looked back to see Officer Kunkle leaning over a desk, blood dripping from his battered face.

"You'd better come with me," Longarm suggested. "They're going to know who set me free, and when that happens, you're a dead man."

"I'm a dead man anyway."

Longarm could hear the riot outside and he wanted to be gone before it was finished. And yet, he knew that he owed his life to this man who wanted to join his brother and become a newspaperman in Gold Hill, Nevada.

"Let's go!" Longarm said, grabbing Kunkle and pulling him toward the door.

"I can't leave my wife and kids!"

"You'll leave them forever if you don't come with me right now!" Longarm argued. "Come on! I promise you we won't go off without your family."

Before Kunkle could answer, Longarm was hurling him outside, then grabbing him and pulling him up the sidewalk, down a dark alley, and out onto another street.

"Where are we going?" Kunkle cried as they heard gunshots begin to erupt behind them.

"As far as we can get from that jail and the gallows," Longarm growled as they half-ran, half-staggered through the dark backstreets of Denver.

Chapter 15

After leaving his jail, Sheriff Belcher had made his tour of the saloons, and in every one of them he was greeted like a celebrity. Glasses were filled and toasts were made to his success in bringing justice in the case of the fallen Marshal Custis Long.

"We all thought that Federal Marshal Custis Long was some kind of knight in shining armor," one very drunk town merchant shouted in the Glass Slipper Saloon and Hotel. "But we know who the *real* knight in shining armor is, and that's our own Sheriff Bert Belcher!"

Everyone cheered and wanted to buy Belcher a drink. And the best part of it was that he'd be an even bigger celebrity tomorrow, shortly after the hanging at one o'clock in the afternoon.

So Belcher decided not to go home and get a few hours of sleep that night. His wife, Agnes, had left him two years ago, taking his two daughters. Which was just fine with the sheriff. Fewer mouths to feed, as far as he was concerned. Agnes had been a thin, high-strung woman who had never stopped complaining about how much her husband drank and how much he seemed to like the saloon girls.

Sheriff Belcher had never told Agnes about his "special protection" business that he ran along with a few of his favorite deputies. And so, while she fretted and fussed constantly over how their family existed on the sheriff's small salary, he had been raking in money for years and putting it into a savings account that no one knew about except Fred Blevins, the mousy little banker over at First Federal Savings. And on top of the money he'd been stashing away, Sheriff Belcher was taking some personal services instead of cash.

"How you doin', honey?"

Sheriff Belcher turned and there was Sally Kingston, the best-looking prostitute in all of Denver. Sally was one of those "personal services" that Belcher enjoyed instead of taking cash payments from the Glass Slipper Saloon and Hotel.

"Why, Sally, I'm just doin' fine tonight," Belcher said, his grin broad and a little lopsided. "And how is your sweet little self?"

"I'm havin' a great time tonight," she said. "Got men waiting in line, but when I heard that you were here I decided I'd come on down and share a drink with you."

"How many men have you had today already?" he asked, feeling a hint of jealousy.

"Oh, honey, I do believe that I lost count about seven o'clock this evening." Sally winked and wiggled her bottom seductively. "But you know that I always have room for *you*."

A couple of men at the bar overheard Sally's comment and laughed out loud until Belcher gave them a hard stare.

"How about it, honey? You interested in a little humpin' tonight with Sally?"

Belcher was drunk, but not so drunk that he couldn't feel his manhood stirring. He leaned close to Sally and whispered, "I ain't gonna stand in no line for you tonight. There are other saloons and other girls that would like me to pay 'em a little visit up in their rooms."

"I know that, honey," she cooed, her hand dropping down to rub his crotch. "But I also know that I'm your *favorite* girl. Now, why don't we skip all this silly talk and go where we can be alone for a few minutes?"

"I figured every room in the place would be sold out, and I ain't interested in humpin' you with customers watchin'."

"Don't you worry about that," Sally assured him, "because I know a secret place where we can be alone for just as long as it takes. Might even be kinda exciting."

Belcher tossed down his whiskey and his voice was hoarse with desire when he said, "Now you really got me curious."

"Then why don't you just buy me a whiskey and follow my sweet ass upstairs!"

"Bartender!" Belcher shouted. "Bring me another and bring one for Sally. The *good* stuff."

"Yes, sir!"

Sally and Belcher had another drink and there was so much noise and revelry that after a half hour Belcher almost forgot about going upstairs with Sally Kingston. But when a crowd was gathered around him and he was laughing and having a good time, Sally grabbed ahold of his gun belt and pulled him along after her, much to the amusement of the crowd.

"Hellfire, Sally. I didn't forget about you."

"Well, you sure acted as if you'd forgotten. So . . . Oh, honey! You all right?"

Belcher had missed a rung on the stairs and fallen flat on his face. He felt like an idiot but fortunately the crowd downstairs was so busy celebrating that no one seemed to notice.

"Honey, are you sober enough to have your way with little Sally tonight?" she asked with real concern.

"Just show me that secret place you have in mind and I'll show you something you'll like a lot."

"I already seen that big thing of yours at least a dozen times," Sally told him as she took his hand and helped him to his feet. "So you just come along now, Sheriff."

Belcher burped and stumbled up the stairs after Sally. His head was spinning and he kept a steady hand on the stair rail so that he didn't miss a step and fall a second time.

When they reached the top of the landing, Belcher knew full well that the first room on the right was rented to Sally Kingston. The next room was where Alice Tucker carried out her busy trade, and then there were Selma and Gloria, and after that he just couldn't remember.

"Well, hello!" Alice Tucker said, exiting her room with the town's new mayor, Hollister White. "Ain't this town on fire!"

"It sure is," Belcher said, for the first time noticing that there were at least five men lined up in the upstairs hallway waiting turns on these girls. "I can see you are all doing a lot of business tonight."

"That we are!" Alice laughed. "I don't think any of us girls are going to get any sleep tonight, but we sure will make some money!"

"Evening, Sheriff," the mayor said to Belcher. "I . . . I

didn't expect to see so many of us lined up for this to-night."

"Evening, Hollister. And I sure didn't expect to see you up here tonight, what with your wife just having had a baby."

The mayor blushed with embarrassment. "Well, I'm trying to lay off of Abby for a few weeks until she . . . uh, you know. Until she recovers from the baby. It was her first and it was a tough delivery."

"That's real thoughtful of you, Hollister." Belcher couldn't hide his sarcasm. "You are one hell of a hus-band."

"Well, thanks," the mayor said. "But all the same, I know that you won't mention this to Abby. She thinks I'm playin' poker this evening with some of the city councilmen."

"Don't you worry about it even a little," Belcher said, not too drunk to make a mental note that this might be something he could use against the man in the near fu-ture. "My lips are sealed."

"Thanks, Sheriff."

"Don't think nothin' of it, Hollister. Is that room empty that you just left? Only take me a few minutes, being the big stud horse that I am."

"Sure, you can use my room," Alice said. "I humped eight men since noon and my pussy is just about ready to snap shut like an overused bear trap. I'm gonna stay downstairs at the bar for at least an hour to give it a chance to revive."

Everyone in the upstairs hallway laughed and Sally pulled Belcher into the room. Surprisingly, Alice's rented room looked about like Sally's, what with it being so small with just a bed, a pitcher of water, a chamber pot, and a chair.

"I thought you were looking forward to a surprise place to do me," Sally said, pouting. "Instead, we wind up in Alice's room."

Belcher raised his eyebrows in question. "Did the 'surprise place' even have a bed?"

"Naw. I was gonna take you out on the fire escape, lift up my skirt, and bend over so you could do me facin' the alley."

"Ha!" Belcher laughed. "And what if someone saw us up there doin' it on the fire escape?"

"They'd probably want to watch it all," Sally told him as she quickly began to undress. "Don't matter to me none."

"Well, I'm kinda drunk but not so drunk that I want to see some deadbeats down in the alley staring up at us going at it."

"Givin' 'em a little show don't hurt none," Sally said, pulling off the last of her clothing and shaking her breasts. "But let's stop all the jabberin'. Time is money for this woman tonight."

Belcher tossed his hat aside, then his coat. He unbuckled his gun belt and then his pants and nearly fell over again when they dropped to his ankles.

"Damn, honey! You've really got a toot on tonight."

"I maybe had more to drink than I thought," he admitted. "But not so much that I can't get 'er up and do your little pussy some real damage. Turn around and bend over!"

Sally just shrugged and did as he ordered, spreading her legs and bending over to lean on the windowsill. Belcher grabbed his manhood and was aghast to discover that it was as soft as an old banana. He squeezed and jerked at himself for a minute or two but nothing was happening.

"What's takin' you so long?" Sally asked, twisting around to look down at his embarrassment. "Why, honey, you ain't ready to do nothin' except maybe piss."

"I'll get there with a little help," he snapped with irritation. "Get down on your knees and do what you know how to do best."

"Okay," she said. "But I sure hope that you can do your part."

"Shut up and suck!"

Sally did as she was told, but after five minutes she was worn out with it and there wasn't any improvement in the situation. "Bert," she whined, "my knees are startin' to hurt and my mouth feels . . . worn out. What's the matter with you tonight?"

This wasn't the first time in his life that Sheriff Bert Belcher had had too much to drink and couldn't get it up. But it had been a while . . . and the last time was with his skinny former wife, and there had been no shame in a man staying small with such an ugly and carpish woman as Agnes. But Sally was good-looking, and she was doing her very best, and nothing was happening for him.

"Damn!" he swore, pulling back from her mouth and just staring in disgust at his floppy, uncooperative member. "I sure don't know what is wrong with it tonight."

"Did you just do some other girl in one of the saloons?"

"Yeah!" Belcher cried, seizing on this excuse to save face. "Yeah, as a matter of fact, I done *two* girls before I came over here to do you."

Sally stomped her foot. "Well, dammit, Bert! Why didn't you tell me so in the first place! I nearly sucked myself to death on you, and all for nothing!"

"I guess I got greedy, and when I saw you I just

wanted to go again," he said with a shrug of his broad shoulders.

Sally started dressing. "Bert, let's just pretend that none of this happened, and you can come back tomorrow night or the next when you're sober and you ain't had a couple of whores already. You know I like you, honey, but for me time is money, and there are a lot of boys out there waitin' to come up and do what you couldn't do tonight."

Belcher's hand shot out and he slapped Sally hard across the side of her head, knocking her to the floor. "Don't you get smart with me!"

She shook her head and tears filled her eyes. "Bert, didn't I do my part? Didn't I do all that I could to make you hard enough?"

"Yeah, but . . ."

"So why'd you go and slap me like that?"

Sheriff Belcher started getting dressed. He was mad at himself for hitting Sally and for not being able to service her even after she gave it such a big effort to make things okay.

"Look," he said, reaching into his pocket and finding some money. "I . . . I'm under a lot of pressure right now. Until we actually get Marshal Custis Long hanging from the end of a rope, I will be on edge."

"That may be so," Sally said, "but it still don't give you the right to hit me so hard. I thought I was your *favorite* whore."

"You are."

"And once you even said maybe we could go off with all that money you've been stashing away and get married. Don't you even remember telling me that, Bert?"

"Well, sure I do. But I sort of got carried away with my mouth that night and . . . well, you know."

"I know," she said, spitting blood into the palm of her hand and then wiping it on a towel. "I didn't really expect you to marry me. But I thought maybe you would."

"Is there anything to drink in here?" Belcher interrupted. "I sure could use another drink."

"There ain't nothin' up here to drink," Sally told him. "It's against the house rules. All the drinkin' has to be done downstairs at the bar."

"Yeah, I know, I know." Sheriff Belcher reached for his hat and then his gun belt. "Look, Sally. Just don't tell anyone about what happened up here tonight."

"Of course, I won't!" She tried to smile but one side of her face was already feeling numb and the smile wasn't working. "I know how embarrassed a man can get when he can't . . . you know, do it. Believe me, Bert, I've seen plenty of men, some a lot younger than you, that had too much to drink and couldn't do anything other than take a piss with their dongs."

"Well, okay then," he said. "We'll just do this another time real soon when I'm feeling better and ain't had two women first."

"I'd like that," she said, not meaning it, and deciding that she would do everything she could not to get with the sheriff when he'd been drinking hard. "I surely would, Bert."

"Okay, then," he said. "Good night, Sally."

"Night, Bert."

"It was a good suck job that you did."

"Thanks."

"Next time."

"Sure, Bert. Next time."

Sheriff Belcher went down the stairs, not meeting anyone's eye and ignoring the calls for him to come and have another free drink. He was feeling bad and then he was feeling even worse when gunfire erupted in the street right in front of his jail and office.

Sheriff Belcher tried to run but he was too drunk. And deep inside, he knew that things had just gone from bad to worse.

Chapter 16

Longarm was taller and leaner and should have been in far better physical shape than poor Officer Dermit Kunkle. However, because of his time in jail with not enough food coupled with no chance to exercise, he was struggling as they ran down alleys and backstreets until they came to Cherry Creek.

"Where are we going?" Kunkle exclaimed.

"I really have no idea," Longarm admitted. "But I expect that half the town is out searching for me. After all, they came for a necktie party, and if they don't get one, they'll be mad as hell."

Kunkle was clinging to a tree for support and trying to catch his breath. "What have I done? Oh, gawd, what have I done?"

"You just saved an innocent man," Longarm reminded the deputy. "And now we're going to have to figure out what to do next."

"I have to get to my family!" Kunkle started to leave but Longarm grabbed the man by the collar.

"Hold up and let's think this out for a minute."

"What is there to think about?" Kunkle shrugged Longarm away. "Sheriff Belcher and all of his deputies will already have figured out that I'm the one who helped you escape."

"That's right," Longarm agreed. "And where is the first place they'll go looking for you?"

"My house," Kunkle said, gulping. "They'll go to my house."

"Exactly," Longarm said. "So that's the *last* place we need to go to right now."

"But . . ."

"Listen to me," Longarm said, his voice taking on a hard edge. "You made a decision to help me, and that was the right decision because we both know that I shot Odell in self-defense. Now, we just have to prove that and get us both off the hook."

"But you were found guilty of murder and sentenced to hang."

Longarm could see that Kunkle was very near the breaking point and was in desperate need of reassurance. "That's true, Dermit. But when a judge is found to be corrupt, then his sentences can be overturned. It's happened plenty of times."

"I've never heard of it happening."

"Well," Longarm said, "trust me. It does happen. And we both know that Judge Henry Henson is in Sheriff Belcher's back pocket and gets paid under the table for taking part in things that he would be disbarred and even imprisoned for doing. Things like taking extortion money or doing the sheriff's bidding when it comes to certain people he is passing sentence upon."

"Yeah, I know that, but how can you prove it?"

"I don't know yet," Longarm admitted. "But consider that we have two very important people now in our corner. The first and most important is Mr. Dunston Crabtree, with all his influence and money."

"Oh, sure, Mr. Crabtree has money but he is from Boston and has no influence whatsoever in Denver."

"But he can hire Denver's best lawyers and investigators. He can use his money to get answers that will come out in a second trial and get me set free. And you saw what his man Reinhold can do."

"Reinhold is probably *dead* by now," Kunkle said morosely.

"If I had to put a bet on it I'd say that Reinhold was probably beaten up pretty badly and tossed into jail. But I doubt that the man is dead, and I'm sure that Mr. Crabtree will have him out on bail by tomorrow."

"What are we going to do?" ' Kunkle asked, his voice pleading.

"We're going to find a safe place to hide until the dust settles."

"But what about my wife and kids?"

"They'll be all right," Longarm assured the man. "Sheriff Belcher and his corrupt deputies aren't stupid enough to harm an innocent woman and her children."

"So you say."

"Listen to me, Dermit. We don't have any choice tonight except to hole up someplace and let things simmer down a mite. When they do, I promise that you will be united with your family and a way will be found to get all of you out of Colorado."

Kunkle's stricken expression took on hope. "As far away as Gold Hill, Nevada?"

"Absolutely," Longarm replied. "You are all going to be on a stagecoach or train by this time next week . . . if not sooner. And when you get to Gold Hill, you won't be busted, either."

"What does that mean?"

"It means that since you saved my life, I'm going to figure out a way to give you three hundred dollars plus some extra so that you and your family can get a fresh start far away from here."

"Don't make promises that you have no chance of keeping," Kunkle said. "I've already had enough of 'em to last a lifetime."

"Three hundred dollars and travel money for you and your family." Longarm stuck out his big hand. "You've got my word on it."

Dermit Kunkle stuck out his smallish hand and they shook. The town deputy squared his shoulders and raised his chin. "All right," he said, "I'll accept your promise and I'll do whatever you say we need to do to get through this shitstorm."

"Glad to hear that," Longarm said, his mind already reaching ahead to the next problem. "I've got a lot of true and loyal friends in Denver. But I don't want to put any more families in danger, so I'm trying to think of a bachelor I know without a doubt can be trusted not to turn us in to Sheriff Belcher."

"I don't know anybody that I could trust that well."

Longarm thought hard for a minute, then snapped his fingers. "I know just the man."

"Who is it?"

"I'll let you know when we get there. Come on, his place isn't all that far from where we're standing."

Longarm broke into a trot. He was shocked at how weak he was after being jailed and he really had to push himself to keep up a steady pace. Thank heavens it was dark and no one could see them as they hurried back into town. There were no more gunshots but the streets were filled with people and every lamp in the downtown area was ablaze.

"This is it," Longarm announced when they came to a back door facing an alley.

"Where are we?"

"We're at Ruben Ortega's Place."

"Isn't that a popular Mexican restaurant?"

"That's right. Ruben makes the best tortillas, salsa, tamales, and tacos this side of the border. The man lost his wife five or six years ago to a cancer and now lives alone in an apartment behind his restaurant. He'll not only be happy to hide us from the law, but he'll feed us so well that I'll be back to my old weight in no time."

"Are you *sure* that he can be trusted? There will be a bounty on your head and a reward for information on mine."

"Ruben is not going to turn us in. He owes me a big favor."

"I hope it's *real* big," Kunkle said as Longarm rapped on the back door to the restaurant.

Almost instantly a voice from inside the building called out, "Who's there?"

"It's Marshal Custis Long. Open up, Ruben!"

The door was unlocked and opened to reveal a handsome man in his early sixties with silver hair and a drooping handlebar mustache. He was wearing an apron heavily dusted with flour.

"Custis!" he cried, throwing out his arms.

Longarm embraced the man and said, "Ruben, we're in a whole barrelful of trouble. This is Deputy Dermit Kunkle and we're being hunted by the sheriff and his deputies."

"I know who this man is, and if he works for Senor Belcher, then he is not to be trusted."

"He helped me to escape from the jail tonight. Without his assistance I would almost surely have hanged tomorrow."

"Come inside and we will talk," Ruben said, glancing up and down the alley. "Sometimes drunks and other men sleep back here at night. If they recognized you they would tell the sheriff in hopes of a reward."

Once they were inside and the door was closed, Ruben led them to a couple of wicker chairs and said, "I'll bet that you are both very hungry. I will get you some food. It will only take a few minutes to heat up beans and tortillas and . . ."

"I could use a drink," Longarm said.

"Tequila or beer?"

"Tequila." Longarm glanced at Kunkle. "What about you?"

"Definitely tequila."

Ruben found them glasses and a bottle of his favorite brand of tequila, then hurried off to prepare them a hot meal. Once he was gone and they'd tossed down a couple shots of the fiery liquor, Kunkle asked, "Are you sure that they won't think to look here for us?"

"I'm sure," Longarm told the man. "The first place they'll look is my apartment, expecting that I'd go there to get my things before heading out of town. Then they'll go to your house and question your wife."

"She won't know anything but she'll be terrified once they tell her that I was the one who helped you to escape."

"But she won't know anything," Longarm reminded the man.

"No, but she'll be so afraid for my life."

"We'll get a message to her that you are all right,"

Longarm said. "Ruben can do that if you give him your address. No one will suspect that he is helping us."

"I hope to god not."

"Okay," Longarm said, thinking aloud. "After they go to my apartment and your house they'll start combing every livery and stable in town, expecting us to try to get horses for our escape. After the stables they'll be searching back alleys and the banks of Cherry Creek through tomorrow morning."

"Everyone in Denver will recognize us both on sight," Kunkle said. "We won't be able to get around."

"I'll ask Ruben to get word to my boss, Billy Vail," Longarm decided. "Billy can then get the wheels of justice moving in the right direction."

"I sure hope so."

Longarm refilled their shot glasses with tequila. "Dermit," he said, "you did a brave thing back there at the jail. Now you just have to have faith that everything is going to work out fine."

"I'll drink to that," Kunkle said.

"Five more minutes!" Ruben Ortega called from up front in the restaurant. "I hope you men are very hungry!"

"I could eat a horse," Longarm said. "And Ruben's food is the best in town."

"I know," Kunkle agreed. "I've been here before."

In five minutes Ruben was hurrying back with two hot plates of tamales, chili peppers, beans, and tortillas. He sat down on his bed and looked at the two fugitives. "Well, Marshal, what is going to happen next?"

"We're going to need your help," Longarm told the man. "But it will put your life in danger if we are caught. You would be jailed along with us and have to go before the judge. He might even sentence you to prison for helping us tonight."

Ruben waved the threat off with one hand and reached for the bottle of tequila with the other. *"Por nada,"* he said. "It is nothing. I lead a very quiet and boring life since my wife, Rosa, passed away. Whatever I can do for you, amigo, I will do gladly."

"That's what I'd hoped to hear," Longarm told the man as he dug into his plate of delicious Mexican food. "And now I'll tell you what I need you to do for us first thing tomorrow morning."

Chapter 17

Ruben Ortega had never been in the all-white section of Denver. He was, after all, a Mexican, and when he was among all white people it was not unexpected for someone to glare at him and sneer, "Remember the Alamo!" But early this Saturday morning, he was on a mission and was very determined. Longarm had given him his boss's address, and now Ruben was standing before the man's house with his hand on the picket fence gate.

Taking a deep breath, he opened the gate and walked up to the house to knock on the door. It was still not yet seven o'clock in the morning and Ruben was sure that the chief United States marshal would be sound asleep.

But the door opened almost immediately and Ruben stepped back, removing his hat and bowing slightly. "Senor Vail?"

"What are you . . . ?" Billy blinked and at once he made the connection. "Come inside, Senor Ortega"

Ruben stepped into the foyer and looked around. The house was too neat and fine, which made him uncomfortable. "I was afraid that maybe I wake you, Senor."

"No. I heard about the jailbreak last night and I haven't slept a wink since. I expected Longarm and that officer might come here looking to hide. But they didn't. What can you tell me?"

"They are safe with me," Ruben said with pride in his voice. "Marshal Long, he asked me to come here and seek your help."

"Anything I can do," Billy said. "Would you like to come into the kitchen and share a cup of coffee?"

"That would be nice. I didn't sleep a wink last night, either."

When they were seated and the coffee had been poured, Billy said, "All right, give me the message and tell me how I can help Custis and that local deputy."

"The marshal says that he needs you to go find Mr. Dunston Crabtree and tell him that he must get that woman who lied about him in court to change her testimony."

"That's going to be very difficult to do," Billy warned. "I already paid a call on Mrs. Crabtree and she stonewalled me. Refused to admit that her husband was killed in self-defense and that she took his gun and either hid or destroyed it."

"Maybe the rich old man from Boston can find a way to make her tell the truth."

"Maybe," Billy Vail agreed. "I understand that his manservant and bodyguard, that big man named Reinhold, is now locked up in jail."

Ruben Ortega shrugged. "I do not know about that. There is one other important thing that Marshal Long needs you to do."

"What?"

"He wants you to give him four hundred dollars."

"Four hundred!"

Ortega shrugged. "It is not for him, Senor Vail; it is for the deputy so he can take his family far away from harm."

"But . . . but four hundred dollars!"

"I am only telling you what the big marshal has asked for."

Billy began to pace back and forth in his small kitchen. "Four hundred is a lot of money."

"Yes, senor. A *lot* of money."

"But it's not so much to give a man for saving you from getting your neck stretched."

"No, senor, it is not so much money for a thing like that."

"And I'll bet that Officer Dermit Kunkle will be willing either to testify at some later date or sign a sworn statement admitting to his perjury in Judge Henson's courtroom."

"No doubt, senor."

"All right then," Billy decided. "I'll find out where Mr. Crabtree is staying in town and then I'll ask the old man to put the screws on Etta. Pay her off or whatever he has to do. And I'll get that four hundred dollars. But tell Custis that I expect it to be paid back someday."

"I will tell him that," Ortega promised.

"Anything else you were supposed to relay along to me?"

" 'Relay'?"

"Yeah, you know. Pass along to me."

"Only that you need to make sure that the deputy's wife and children are protected. Deputy Kunkle, he is very afraid for them."

"And he probably should be," Billy said. "Yes, I'll get several of the deputies from my office to start a twenty-four-hour watch over the family. And then I'd like to visit Custis. I'll figure out a way to do it without putting you in danger, Mr. Ortega."

"He will not be staying with me much longer. The marshal said that he will be leaving my place very soon."

"Did he say where he would go to hide next?"

Ortega shook his head. "Only he asked me to make many tortillas for him and Senor Kunkle so they can hide without having to worry about food."

Billy Vail almost smiled. "And I'll just bet anything that Custis also asked you to include a few bottles of whiskey to wash all those tortillas down."

"He did but I told him I could only give him beer or tequila."

"That damned Custis will drink anything so long as it's not milk or water."

Both men laughed and then sat down to have a quick cup of coffee.

Billy Vail's mind was racing. He couldn't stop thinking about how this was all going to unfold. But there was no time to waste fretting and worrying. Longarm had told him what needed to be done next, and Billy knew that everything hinged on it being done fast.

Chapter 18

Longarm and Dermit Kunkle were eating a monstrous breakfast of scrambled eggs, hot sauce, and pork sausage when Ruben slipped in the back door of his establishment and joined them.

"Well," Longarm asked around a mouthful of food, "how'd it go?"

"It went fine. I went right to Senor Vail's house and no one stopped me or said a word."

"That's because it was so early on a Saturday morning that everyone in Billy's neighborhood was probably still sleeping," Longarm reflected. "Tell me what Billy said about that four hundred dollars I need for Dermit and his family."

"He said that it was a lot of money and I agreed. But then he said it was not so much money if a man saved you from hanging and he was willing to either change his testimony in a Denver court, or . . ."

"Now wait a minute!" Kunkle cried, jumping up from the table. "I can't come back here to testify! Marshal, even if you do manage to bring down Sheriff Belcher and

Judge Henson, his deputies will never forgive me for turning on their boss. No, sir! They'll put an end to me, and you can count on that sure as tomorrow is Sunday."

Longarm knew that Kunkle was right. "Okay," he said, "calm down a minute."

"May I say what else Senor Vail told me?" Ortega asked.

"Sure," Longarm said.

"He says that this man could testify or he could sign some papers under oath that he did not tell the truth in Judge Henson's court. Senor Vail said that would be good enough to clear your name."

"See there, Dermit?" Longarm offered. "You could go before a judge in Nevada and sign a paper swearing that you had lied in your testimony against me. And that would be sufficient."

"You really think so?"

"I'm sure of it," Longarm told the man. "Maybe not as things stand right now, but after we get Etta to tell the truth, your sworn and written statement would be the final nail in Sheriff Belcher's coffin."

"Marshal Long, I helped you to escape from jail. Isn't that enough? Now I just want to be shut of all this trouble and never hear from anyone about you, Etta Crabtree, or her dead husband ever again," Kunkle told him, with a shake of his head.

"I'm sorry, but that simply isn't good enough," Longarm said quietly. "You're going to have to see this out to the end. Dermit, my life and my reputation hang in the balance. If you'd have told the truth right from the start in Henson's court, I wouldn't have been sent to jail in the first place nor sentenced to hang."

"Oh, yes, you would have," Kunkle argued. "The judge and the sheriff had already put the noose around your neck, only you just didn't know it at the time. Sheriff Belcher hates you and all federal officers. He was always complaining and trashing you people. So when you got in that mess with Mrs. Crabtree and shot her husband . . . it was exactly the kind of thing the sheriff had been hoping for and prayin' would happen."

"Okay," Longarm said. "I agree. And I've admitted that I made a stupid mistake. But I'm not going to hang for it, nor am I going to be stripped of my office as a federal marshal or have a black mark on my record. And *you* are the one who is going to make sure that doesn't happen."

"And if I can't?"

"Then we will give you and your family only a one-way train ticket to Reno. That's it. As hard as this may sound, if you won't help me out and clear the record, the Kunkle family will all *walk* to Gold Hill dead broke. No money for food and no money for a partnership with your brother in his newspaper. Is that the way you want to join your brother? Penniless and with your hands out begging?"

"Of course not!"

"If you want that four hundred dollars you're gonna see this out to the end," Longarm said in a hard, flat voice that brooked no argument.

Kunkle threw his head back and stared up at the ceiling for a long time before he finally sighed and returned to his breakfast. "All right. I'll do what you ask."

"Good!" Longarm was thinking hard. "We'll have the one-way tickets ready for you and your family to take the next train out of town. Do you or your wife have any cash stashed away?"

"A few dollars. Maybe thirty or forty at most."

"That will carry you to Nevada and get you all on

a coach up to the Comstock Lode where your brother lives," Longarm said. "Once you sign a sworn statement before a Nevada judge that you lied in court testimony because you and your family were threatened by death from Sheriff Belcher, I'll telegraph you the balance of the four hundred."

"And I have your solemn word on that?" Kunkle asked.

"Hell, yes! And do I have your word that you will do what I've asked as soon as you reach Nevada?"

"Yes," Kunkle said. "You have my word."

"Then let's shake on it, and if everything goes as planned, the next train leaving Denver is on Monday morning. It will take you and your family up to Cheyenne and you'll switch trains and ride all the way to Reno. From Reno there are mail and passenger coaches leaving every day for Virginia City and Gold Hill."

"When will we arrive there?"

Longarm considered the question. "If the travel goes smoothly and the trains are all on schedule, you and your family will be having breakfast in Gold Hill by Thursday."

"Thursday," Kunkle said, closing his eyes to visualize the place and the time where he at last had a chance to make a future for his family. "My god, I can hardly believe it could all happen."

"It *will* happen," Longarm promised, winking at Ruben Ortega before smacking his lips and digging back into his Mexican omelet.

Billy Vail entered Denver's plush three-story Huntington Hotel less than an hour after Ruben Ortega's hurried and secretive visit to his home. He had been in this hotel many times when high-ranking dignitaries from Washington, D.C., had visited the outlands of the West, and so he knew his way around the place and was recognized by the desk clerk.

"I need to see Mr. Dunston Crabtree."

The desk clerk said, "Mr. Crabtree is already having breakfast in the dining room. Is he . . . uh, expecting you this morning, Marshal Vail?"

"No, but he'll be very interested in what I have to say."

"It must have something to do with that wild jailbreak that your deputy made last night. Is it true that one of Sheriff Belcher's own deputies helped Marshal Long escape, along with Reinhold?"

"I can't comment on that. Excuse me," Billy said, moving across the chandeliered lobby with its plush carpeting and impressive statues and original oil paintings.

Dunston P. Crabtree sat alone at a table in the corner of the elegant dining room. He did not wish for company, nor did he wish to be disturbed, for he had already learned that Reinhold was in jail and in some considerable pain from a beating he'd taken during the jailbreak. Crabtree had also been informed that three of the sheriff's men had been sent to the hospital and another was unable to speak or eat because of a broken jaw. All the top doctors in Denver except one were attending to the serious injuries inflicted by Reinhold, and that exception was Dr. Andrews, the best of them all, who was right now attending to Crabtree's manservant and bodyguard.

"Uh, excuse me, Mr. Crabtree?"

The old man didn't bother to turn around. "If you're a reporter looking for a story, then go away."

"I'm the senior federal marshal in Denver. Perhaps you've seen me in court and . . ."

Crabtree wiped his lips and laid down his fork. He turned slowly and said, "Of course. You are Chief United States Marshal William Vail and you've come to seek my help for your deputy marshal, Custis Long."

"That's right."

"Please sit down and join me for breakfast. Have you eaten yet, Marshal Vail?"

"No."

Crabtree didn't even call or glance at the formally attired waiter. He simply pointed at Billy and the waiter went into action. "This hotel really does serve quite a good breakfast and dinner. However, their lunch leaves much to be desired."

"I always thought it was pretty special . . . when I felt I could afford the three dollars."

Crabtree allowed himself a thin smile. "So, Marshal Vail, we have much to talk about and to do this morning."

"Yes, sir."

"What are you going to do?"

Billy waited until the waiter had poured him a cup of what he knew would be wonderful coffee and left them to speak privately. That done, he quickly told the rich man from Boston what Longarm desired for himself and for Officer Kunkle.

Crabtree waited until Billy was served a huge breakfast and then he continued to eat. The old man had an amazing appetite for a man his size and age.

When Billy Vail finished, Dunston Crabtree sipped the last of his coffee, ate the last crust of his French pastry, and said, "I won't help you with the money for the deputy who committed perjury. I simply cannot reward a liar, and that has always been my practice. However, I fully agree that Etta has to be made to tell the truth."

"But how?" Billy asked. "You just said that you never reward a liar, and Etta Crabtree's outrageous lies on the witness stand are the sole reason my best and most trusted deputy has been sentenced to hang."

"Yes," Crabtree agreed. "That is the problem, is it not? How do I make Etta tell the truth and probably put herself behind bars without paying her off? Without giving her a reward for her shameless dishonesty?"

Billy shrugged. "Beats me."

"I have been thinking about that dilemma all morning," Crabtree confessed. "To be honest, I have *always* loathed Etta. I knew that she was scum and trash when my son met and fell in love with her. I also knew that she was after my money and that, given the opportunity, she would do anything and everything in her power to gain my considerable wealth."

Billy started to speak, but the Bostonian raised a slender forefinger. "Marshal Vail, you most assuredly have seen many unsavory characters in your career. Is that not so?"

"is," Billy offered. "I've seen the very worst of mankind."

"And womankind?" Crabtree asked.

"I've seen a few bad women. Not bad in terms of the ones that are working as prostitutes. I have always had more pity or compassion for an honest, hardworking whore. Half of them were raped and abused as girls. Most came from the most wretchedly poor circumstances you can imagine, and very few have any education or other realistic means of supporting themselves. In the West, it is very much a man's world and the only so-called 'good women' are those respectably married, widowed, or those who chose to be churchgoing spinsters and schoolteachers."

"I see."

"Etta probably came from a very bad background and she has had to scratch, claw, and fight her way all through life. I can only imagine what she must have felt when she landed the only son of a very wealthy man from Boston and soon learned that the son had been rejected."

Crabtree raised his eyebrows in question. "'Rejected'?"

"Well, didn't you reject Odell as your son and the heir to your considerable fortune?"

"Ahhh, that is a harsh choice of words, Marshal. My wife and I did reject him from our close Boston circle of friends and associates, but only after he proved to be . . . uh, undisciplined and untrustworthy. And even when we sent him west to your city we did buy him that apartment building and help support him for many years. When he and Etta last visited, we of course paid for all his travel, and what did my son then do in return?"

The old man shook his head and his voice quivered with outrage. "Odell repaid us by *stealing* my wife's . . . his own dear mother's . . . finest jewelry! And he tried desperately to extract all the money from our bank account. Failing that, he managed to appropriate a painting that was worth a small fortune. And he sold it for a mere four hundred dollars!"

Billy nodded and suddenly became worried that the old man might have heart failure right here at the table because he was getting so angry. "Sir, I did not come here to dredge up old bad feelings and betrayals by your late son. I came here to ask you to help my deputy, Custis Long."

"By going to the woman who helped Odell steal from me and my wife."

"Yes, sir."

Crabtree expelled a deep sigh and his eyes were clouded with pain. "All right," he said at last. "You must have considered that I already helped your deputy escape by having Reinhold take on the sheriff's men. In fact, he was pretending to be dead drunk so that he would be tossed into jail and then could help your marshal make his escape. So I have obviously already committed to helping your marshal."

"I'm curious, Mr. Crabtree. How was Reinhold going to break not only himself but also my deputy out of that heavily guarded jail?"

"I would rather not say. It's not important anymore, but we had devised a rather ingenious plan so that once Reinhold was in one of the jail cells he would have had the means to break out and free Custis Long. Trust me, the plan would have been successful. However, when that liar Kunkle acted, it threw our plans out the jail cell window, so to speak."

"And so Reinhold put up a fight long enough to allow them to escape."

"Exactly so," Crabtree said with obvious pride. "Unfortunately, Reinhold was overwhelmed not only by the deputies but also by some of the drunken mob that had collected out in the street. And so now the poor man requires medical attention."

"As do the deputies that he nearly destroyed."

Crabtree chuckled. "Yes, that motley band of corrupt bastards!"

"So that brings us back to Etta."

"It does indeed. No, Marshal Vail, I will not reward her for her vile dishonesty and betrayal. I will instead seek other means to persuade her to do the right and honest thing, thereby recanting her testimony. But first, Judge Henry Henson must be removed from his bench and disbarred so that he cannot again violate his oath and the law of this land."

"You can get the judge removed from the bench?"

"I think so. It is not going to be easy, and it has already taken more time than anticipated, but that is my determined goal. He must be taken down or he will ruin any hopes we have of making a great wrong . . . right."

"What can I do to help?"

"I must meet with Custis Long today."

"That might not be possible."

"It *must* be possible," Dunston Crabtree insisted. "And you will make it happen."

Billy Vail found himself nodding. "All right," he agreed. "I'll find a way to do it."

"I knew that you would," Crabtree told him. "Now, would you care for a cigar and a stroll about town? I'm sure that it will be a most interesting stroll."

"I'd like nothing better," Billy said truthfully.

"Good, then finish more excellent coffee and let's be out and about your wild and wicked western town!"

Chapter 19

Longarm and Kunkle were seated on overturned empty pickle barrels, eating another sumptuous Mexican meal, when both Billy Vail and Dunston Crabtree slipped in to join them.

"Smells good," the wealthy old man said. "Mind if I have a plate?"

Ruben Ortega beamed. "Of course, Senor Crabtree. I have plenty for everyone."

"In that case," Billy said, "I'll also take a plate."

Soon, they were all eating at a small table, and when the meal was over, Longarm looked at the rich man from Boston and said, "How is your man Reinhold?"

"He's pretty battered and he's locked up in that damned jail, but I've got an excellent doctor attending to him. All the other doctors in town are working on Sheriff Belcher's thugs."

"I'm sorry about Reinhold," Longarm said. "Please tell him how much I appreciate his help. Without him coming to our sides, I'd be back in jail . . . or dead."

"I'll convey your appreciation," Crabtree promised. "But now we have to plan our next move."

"And that would be?" Longarm asked.

"Why, it would be against Etta, of course. Then the sheriff, and finally that corrupt Judge Henson."

Longarm smiled. "Why in that particular order?"

Crabtree wiped refried beans from his lips with a silk handkerchief and said, "I believe Etta is the key. If we can get her to recant her false testimony, all the rest falls into place."

"That's right," Billy said in agreement.

Longarm looked from one man to the other. "So, Mr. Crabtree, have you decided to pay her off?"

"Hell, no!" Crabtree exclaimed. "You're going to scare her out of her wits! Put the fear into her so bad that she won't be able to wait to testify that she lied in your trial and that you shot Odell in self-defense."

"And just how," Longarm asked, "am I supposed to put that much fear in a woman who is as hard and calculating as Etta?"

The old man shrugged his narrow shoulders. "I should think that you have had experience in such matters. After all, you are the renowned law officer . . . the one who has a reputation for ensuring that justice is fairly served."

Longarm got up from his seat and frowned. "All right," he said. "But it's not in my nature to be unkind or frightening to women."

"This is *not* a woman," Kunkle said, with bitterness choking his voice. "It is a lying, conniving *bitch* who was more than happy to perjure herself so that she could gain Mr. Crabtree's fortune even though it meant you had to hang."

"Is she still living at her apartment?"

"As far as I know," Billy answered.

"Not so," Crabtree told them. "After the shooting, Etta immediately moved into the Huntington Hotel where I'm staying. She did so in order to try to win me over. She has been pestering me incessantly in the vain hope that I'll forgive her and take her back to Boston with me."

Longarm nodded. "But you're not going to do that."

"Of course not!" Crabtree snapped. "Why would I allow a deadly parasite into the sanctity of my home?"

"What room is Etta staying in?" Longarm asked.

"Room 104."

"Does she have anyone staying with her?" Longarm wanted to know.

Crabtree thought about that for a moment. "I don't think so. She is trying to convince me that she actually loved Odell and will mourn for him forever."

"I'll visit Etta tonight," Longarm told them. "And I'll do what is necessary to make her agree to change her testimony."

Billy Vail looked skeptical. "Can you *really* do it?"

"I can't afford to fail," he said, looking around the little table. "Either she recants or I get hanged."

"Don't let her scream," Dunston Crabtree advised. "Every room in the hotel is full and the walls aren't all that thick."

"I won't let her scream," he vowed. "But neither will I leave her until she swears that she will tell the truth."

"Get that in writing," Billy suggested.

"Good idea," Longarm said. "But I sure don't look forward to seeing that woman again."

The truth was that he really, really didn't *ever* want to see Etta Crabtree again. He despised that scheming, lying witch. However, life was often about having to do things that were difficult and disgusting.

And this, Longarm knew, was going to be one of them.

"I shall be going now," Crabtree told them. "Should I go out the front or the back way into the alley?"

"Go through the alley," Longarm decided. "Billy, you should wait five minutes and do the same."

"I will."

At the back door, Crabtree turned before leaving and said, "I'm going to find the best attorney in Denver and start working on Judge Henson. Can you recommend someone?"

"William Martin is about as good an attorney as you can find but he's probably all booked up and he's very expensive."

"I'll make it worth his while to help me bring down the judge," Crabtree promised. "Meanwhile, Marshal Vail, perhaps you ought to pay a visit to Sheriff Belcher and see if you can rattle his cage a bit."

"My pleasure," Billy said.

"All right then," Longarm said. "Let's all meet up here first thing tomorrow morning and compare notes. If we've done our jobs, something good should start happening right away."

"I hope so," Dermit Kunkle fretted. "Because I'd like to see my wife and get the hell out of this town."

"It will happen," Longarm promised the nervous former lawman. "If you just keep your nerve up and give us another day . . . maybe two . . . everything will turn out right and you'll be on that train for Nevada."

Kunkle swallowed hard and nodded his head as the three men stared at him, wondering if he could even be trusted to do as he was told.

Early that evening, Longarm had gotten a key from Dunston Crabtree to Room 104 and he hadn't bothered to ask the old Bostonian how he'd come into its possession. Now, Longarm pressed an ear to Etta Crabtree's door and listened carefully for any noise inside. He wasn't expecting there to be anyone else in the room except Etta, and he had no earthly idea how he was going to scare or force her into changing her testimony and admitting that he'd shot her enraged husband in self-defense.

Longarm gently inserted the key into her door lock and turned it, then softly pushed the door open. He was hoping that Etta Crabtree was either drunk or asleep and that he could take her by surprise and put a gag in her big mouth before she could scream.

The room was dark and he pulled the door shut behind him, then stood and tried to let his eyes adjust to the poor light. The window in Etta's room was open and a soft breeze rustled the white lacy curtains. Longarm finally was able to see the outline of the woman lying on her bed.

He tiptoed across the room and stood over her for a moment, then he pulled back the covers and leaned forward, prepared to stuff the rag that he had brought into her mouth.

Only she wasn't breathing. Etta Crabtree was bleeding and there was a short dagger buried to the hilt between her large breasts.

"Holy shit!" Longarm breathed, recoiling.

Suddenly, a figure just outside the room stuck a shotgun through Etta's open window. Longarm dove for the floor just as two blasts filled the hotel room. Half of Etta's head was suddenly gone, as was whoever had fired the murderous shotgun blast.

Longarm heard the sound of feet running down the boardwalk outside and he heard more running down the hotel hallway. He knew in an instant that if he were caught in this room, no matter what Dunston Crabtree or anyone else said, he was going to hang.

Without a moment's hesitation, Longarm dove through the open window, struck the boardwalk, and came to his feet running. Someone had outsmarted him and his friends, and now he was in even more of a mess than he had been already . . . though that seemed almost impossible.

Chapter 20

The lamplight along West Colfax Avenue was poor but sufficient for Longarm to see a man running hard toward the capitol building with its huge gold dome. Longarm figured that the man was going to cut across the grass and through the trees and gardens that made up the capitol grounds, and then perhaps make his way toward Cherry Creek, where there was even more cover for hiding or ambushing.

Anticipating his direction, Longarm cut west across the corner of the grounds, running as hard as his long legs would allow. He had been faster in his youth, but he could still cover a lot of territory in a hurry with his long strides. He saw a dark figure dodging through trees and emerging on the street not fifty yards ahead. Because Longarm knew the man was Etta's murderer, he wanted to take him alive, if at all possible.

But when the man rounded a corner and disappeared for a moment, Longarm figured he had better slow down, catch his breath, and ease around that corner or he might be stepping into another blast from the double-barreled shotgun.

So he stopped at the edge of the capitol grounds, drew his gun, and walked slowly, trying to catch his breath and stay in the shadows. Overhead there was a half-moon and some dark clouds that covered most of the starlight.

Approaching the corner of the brick building where the killer had disappeared, Longarm unholstered his Colt and cocked back the hammer. Taking a deep breath and ducking low, he moved quickly, expecting an ambush. But he was mistaken, and far up the street he could see the receding silhouette of the assassin.

Longarm took off running again. He knew that he was faster than the man he chased, but after being in jail so long he was not nearly as strong or fit as usual. Still, he was catching up to the man, and if he didn't lose him in some alley or between the buildings, he thought he still had an excellent chance of overtaking and capturing his quarry.

"Stop!" Longarm shouted. "You are under arrest!"

The assassin shouted something over his shoulder and kept running, but his speed had slowed dramatically. Longarm took off after him again, gun in hand.

When the assassin heard the fast pounding of Longarm's boots on the pavement, he stopped, spun around, and dropped to his left knee as he lifted and aimed the shotgun.

Longarm dove over a water trough for horses just as the shotgun unleashed its deadly power into the trough. Water erupted into the sky and wood splinters dug into Longarm in a dozen places as he hugged the wet ground.

"Damn you!" Longarm cursed, hearing the man break open the shotgun to reload. "You ain't gonna get a third chance at me with that shotgun!"

Longarm jumped up and started firing just as fast as he could pull his trigger. The big pistol in his hand bucked and belched smoke and fire, and the man with the shotgun began to stagger backward in jerky steps. When he came up against a building, Longarm shot him dead in the chest with his last two unspent rounds.

"Well," Longarm said, more to himself than the dead man, "I guess that damn sure means that Ike Reedy won't be putting any noose around my neck."

Chapter 21

Longarm went to see a doctor he knew and trusted so that the man could pick all the splinters out of his poor carcass.

"You're damn lucky a couple of these splinters didn't take out both of your eyes," the doctor grumped as he dug yet another wicked piece of wood out of Longarm's flesh. "What the hell happened? You get caught in a buzz saw?"

"No, I just got overly well acquainted with a shotgun and a horse-watering trough," Longarm replied.

"You must know that half the town is hunting for you and there is a bounty on your head for a thousand dollars . . . dead or alive."

"That much, huh?"

"I could almost retire with a thousand dollars," the doctor said, giving Longarm a wink. "I'd have to dig out a hundred bullets and a thousand more splinters, plus deliver about fifty babies and sew maybe five hundred stitches to get that much money."

"Doc," Longarm said, "you ain't cut out to do anything but be an honest friend and fine physician. Besides, a thousand dollars all at once would probably send you to the saloon and whorehouse, and you'd wind up in an even worse mess than I'm in."

"I'm sure you're right," the old doctor said, "but it might be fun for a little while."

"It wouldn't be," Longarm said. "Trust a man who knows."

"You sure are in a terrible fix. I thought you'd be hanged by old Ike Reedy by now."

"He ain't going to ever hang anyone else in this world," Longarm said. "Ike is the one who tried to blow me to smithereens tonight. He also murdered Etta Crabtree in her bed. Looked like he probably raped and strangled the woman before burying a dagger in her chest."

"Holy cow!" the doctor said, whistling. "Etta Crabtree is dead?"

"At the Huntington Hotel, although her body is still warm. I went to see her and try to make her change her false testimony against me, but I'm betting Sheriff Belcher figured I'd do that, and he had Ike waiting to blast me with his shotgun."

"So they're both dead and you look like you wrestled a porcupine."

"That's about the size of it, Doc."

"What happens to you next? I tell you, Custis, your life is far more exciting than those cheap dime novels of the West that I can't help but buy and read."

"Glad you find me exciting. How much longer?"

"Do you want all the splinters out . . . or just the ones longer than a bullet?"

"Just the big ones. I don't want someone to find me here or it might still go hard on you, Doc. Besides that,

I've taken about all the abuse that I'm going to take, and it's time to go after the last two assholes still standing."

"And they would be?"

"Sheriff Bert Belcher and Judge Henry Henson. Who else?"

"You gonna kill them?" the doctor asked, digging another splinter out of Longarm's shoulder.

"If I do, it will be after they confess that they set me up and are both as crooked as a dog's hind leg. I want them sent to prison for a long time."

"The judge going to prison? Somehow I can't see that happening."

"Oh, you'll see it, all right," Longarm pledged. "Just get me patched up and on my way. And don't sleep in too late tomorrow morning or you might miss the rest of the show."

"I'd tag along if I could," the doc told him. "But I'd just slow you down and I want to be here in case I have to dig more splinters or lead out of your poor carcass."

"That sounds like the right thing to do, Doc. How much do I owe you?"

The doctor waved a hand of dismissal. "If you make it, you can pay me two dollars. If you don't make it, I will at least have one hell of a good and exciting story to tell my kids and grandchildren."

"Fair enough, Doc!"

Longarm headed back out into the night. He could hear men shouting and he guessed that two murders—one of a woman in her bed and the other the most infamous hangman in Colorado—were causing quite a stir on top of everything else that was happening tonight in Denver.

He was going back to Ruben Ortega's Place to make

sure that Dermit Kunkle was still holding steady. Also, it was the only place that he felt safe right now and knew that he could get some damn good food to eat at this late and desperate hour.

Chapter 22

Longarm and Dermit Kunkle were both dozing in their chairs when Billy Vail and Dunston Crabtree knocked softly on the back door of Ruben Ortega's Place. Ruben hurried to the door and whispered, "Who is there?"

"It's us, Ruben. Open up!"

When the two men were inside and the door to the alley was locked, Longarm said, "What is going on?"

"That's what we want to know!" Crabtree cried, for the first time looking his actual years and seemingly rattled. "Etta was murdered in her hotel bed and then a little later the whole town went crazy when they found the hangman, Ike Reedy, shot to death over on Colfax! I'm telling you, everyone in Denver is half-crazed and in a murderous panic."

"Oh my gawd," Kunkle wailed. "I've got to get to my family and make sure they are protected."

Before anyone could stop the former deputy, Kunkle bolted out of the door and into the alley and took off running.

"Let him go," Longarm said. "We can get his written statement tomorrow and he'll freely give it."

"How do you know that?" Billy asked, looking very worried.

"I just know that he will no longer be afraid of either Judge Henson or Sheriff Belcher, because we are going to make sure they are both disgraced, stripped of their offices, and forever done with this town."

Billy threw up his hand in question. "That all sounds just fine, but how in the world can . . ."

Longarm raised his hands for silence. "Listen well, both of you. I went to see Etta after you gave me her room key, Mr. Crabtree. Someone had gotten to her only a few minutes before I did. They raped her . . . probably so people would think I savaged the woman again out of revenge . . . and then they stabbed her to death. And that someone was waiting to ambush me with a shotgun poking through her open hotel window."

Billy's jaw dropped. "Ike Reedy did Etta in?"

"That's right." Longarm pulled up his bloodstained shirt. "And he would have killed me if I hadn't dived behind Etta's bed and then a stout water trough. He pulled double triggers on me twice and I got lucky."

"You don't look so lucky," Crabtree said with skepticism. "Your face is a mess and your clothes are all bloodstained."

"I'm *alive*," Longarm told the old man. "And for the moment, that feels real good. So how did it go with Judge Henson?"

Dunston Crabtree shook his head. "I hired that lawyer you recommended and told him everything we know and then we went to see the judge at his hotel. Henson had a couple of tough men standing beside him and he insisted they stay there while we talked."

"Let me guess what happened," Longarm said. "Judge Henson spit in your eye and told you to stick your thumb up your ass."

"That's right." Crabtree snorted in anger. "He told me and our lawyer to get the hell out of his sight. He's a tough sonofabitch and he's not about to panic or buckle under threats."

Longarm hadn't been expecting any good news about Hanging Judge Henson, and so he turned to Billy. "Did you speak to Sheriff Belcher?"

"No, he wasn't at his office. I looked in on Reinhold and warned Belcher's deputies if anything more happened to him, I would see that they all ended up in a federal prison."

"Thanks for doing that," Crabtree said with relief. "I'm going to get Reinhold out of that stinking jail one way or another."

"Let it wait until tomorrow," Longarm said, "because we're going to wrap this up by daybreak come hell or high water."

"If anyone recognizes you out on the streets tonight," Billy Vail warned, "they'll set up a howl that the people in Pueblo will be able to hear, and they'll open up on you as if you were General Santa Anna storming the Alamo."

"I won't give anyone that chance," Longarm promised. "Billy, lend me your hat and coat."

"They won't nearly fit," Billy warned.

His boss was right. "Mr. Crabtree, we're almost the same height. Can I burrow that expensive dove-gray Stetson and your fine overcoat?"

"Of course, but Marshal Vail and I insist on coming along with you wherever you go tonight."

"Thanks, but no thanks," Longarm told them. "Billy,

you have way too much to lose if I fail, and Mr. Crabtree, you wouldn't do well in prison . . . no slight intended."

"None taken," the wealthy man said, "but . . ."

"I'm going to find Sheriff Belcher and I'm going to
make sure that Judge Henson and he reach an agreement."

"And that would be?" Crabtree asked.

"That the sheriff immediately resigns from his office
and the judge resigns from his bench. Also, they both
must admit in writing that I was framed, and leave Denver forever with nothing but the shirts on their backs. No
horses to ride, no trains or coaches, either. They are going to leave Denver on foot without even a damned dollar in their pockets."

"They'll *never* do that!" Billy exclaimed.

"I won't give them any choice but to leave broke and
in disgrace . . . or die," Longarm said flatly. "And when I
make sure they understand that is their one and only
choice, I think they'll prove smart enough to quit and
run."

The man from Boston and Billy Vail exchanged worried glances, then Crabtree removed his handsome Stetson and gave it to Longarm before shrugging out of his
coat.

"If you fail," Crabtree said, "I will be very sorry about
it, but I will get my friend Reinhold and return to Boston."

"As well you should," Longarm told him.

"He won't fail," Billy insisted. "Custis Long always
gets done what he sets out to do."

"I hope and pray that is so," Crabtree said. "But even if
not, I have to say this trip to Denver has been one of the
most remarkable adventures of my entire life, and you
gentlemen can be sure that I've had more than my share."

"You call it an 'adventure,'" Longarm said. "That's a pretty soft term for what I would call a disaster."

"Ah," the Bostonian said, "but you do have to admit that you have learned a great deal from all of this misfortune that has been heaped upon you."

"I have at that," Longarm conceded. "Namely to stay away from married women, no matter if they promise to substantially reduce my rent for a poke or two on Sunday mornings."

Crabtree allowed himself a smile and Longarm winked at Billy Vail, who tried to smile.

"Senor Long," Ruben Ortega said. "Excuse me for interrupting this important talk, but I have some tortillas and frijoles heating on the stove up front and wondered if you would like a last meal. It would be my honor, senor."

Longarm pulled on Crabtree's coat, which was a bit tight but would have to do for just a little while. He then clamped a hand on Ruben's strong shoulder and said, "When the dust settles and this passes, I will make sure that everyone in the federal building eats lunch here at least once a week."

"Senor, that would be such a blessing! But how could I handle so many people?"

"If this works out," Dunston Crabtree said, "I will buy you a bigger restaurant and more tables for all the help you have given us and the risk to your own life you have taken in the service of justice."

Ruben Ortega beamed, then he bowed slightly and went off to his kitchen to start preparing for his breakfast customers.

Chapter 23

Longarm knew where Sheriff Belcher called home. It was a little house located two blocks behind the Denver Mint that was remarkable only in that it was unkempt, with peeling paint and a picket fence that was falling apart. Longarm's railroad pocket watch had been confiscated by the sheriff's deputies, who had probably either sold it or pawned it away. No matter. Longarm glanced up at the fading moon and stars and he knew that dawn was only a few minutes away. He would have to move swiftly, and he would have to be very forceful and persuasive.

Well and good. Forceful was very much to his liking this cool, gray morning as he checked the big Colt revolver on his left hip. He had waited a long, long time to get his revenge on Sheriff Bert Belcher and rid the town of his pestilence.

Longarm didn't hesitate for even a moment as he kicked the rickety gate off its hinges and strode right up to Sheriff Belcher's front door. He tried the handle, and, as expected, it was locked. Longarm reared back and kicked the door so hard that it crashed inward. His gun was out and he was moving fast through the door.

Sheriff Belcher was not alone. He was sleeping with a mousy prostitute named Candy, and there was just enough light coming through the bedroom window to see that they both had their mouths hanging open and were snoring in unison. An empty bottle of whiskey was lying on the floor and Longarm almost tripped over it on his way across their littered and cramped bedroom.

"Hey, asshole!" Longarm stormed, tearing the covers off the pair. "This is *your* judgment day!"

The sheriff groaned and tried to sit up, so Longarm punched him full in the face and put him back down again. The prostitute wailed in terror and Longarm grabbed her arm and helped her out of the bed.

"Grab your clothes and get out of here, fast!" he ordered.

The whore was so frightened that she got out of the house fast, without a stitch of clothing.

Belcher groaned and then he sat up to spit blood on his bedspread. "Sonofabitch!" he swore, blinking and wheezing. "Sonofabitch!"

Longarm reached down, grabbed Belcher by the balls, and crushed them like soft grapes. The man screamed and threw his flabby arms up in the air as if he were praising the Lord. Longarm twisted the sheriff's balls like a wet dishrag and Belcher screamed even louder.

"Get up, you corrupt bastard!" Longarm ordered, finally releasing his hold. "Get up and march out of this house or I'll blow you straight to hell!"

"Oh, sweet Jaysus! Don't kill me," Belcher groaned, cupping his crotch. "Oh, please don't do that again!"

"Get up and move!"

The sheriff of Denver staggered out of his bed and

tried to grab his clothes but Longarm kicked him in his bare, fat ass and sent him reeling toward the front door.

"This will sure as hell make some tongues wag, what with you and that whore both out on the street naked as the day you were born. Now hurry along, because we're going to visit your best and most rotten friend, Judge Henry Henson!"

Ten minutes later, and with some people just beginning to stir and then gawk, Longarm marched the sheriff through the Blue Dog Saloon and then into the fine Cody Hotel, which was owned by the judge and the sheriff, thanks to all the extortion they'd enjoyed.

"Which room is the judge staying in?" Longarm demanded.

The desk clerk, who had been sleeping in his chair, jumped a foot or more and then stammered, "Room one. First door on the left past the fireplace."

"Good!"

"You want me to wake him?"

"Hell, no. Give me a key and I'll have that pleasure for myself," Longarm growled, sticking his hand out. "But I want you along to witness what happens next."

"But . . ."

"Get your lazy ass around that desk and follow us so you can tell people what happened here this fine morning."

"Yes, sir!"

Longarm was angry and he jabbed his gun's barrel into Sheriff Belcher's spine and sent him staggering across the impressive hotel lobby. "You heard the clerk, first door on the left. But then I'm sure you know it well."

"Listen," Belcher pleaded, trying to walk bowlegged

because his balls were still on fire. "Maybe a mistake has been made and we . . ."

"Shut up and keep moving!"

When they got to the door, Longarm said, "Put the key in the lock and open it!"

Belcher took the key and his hand was shaking as he inserted it into the lock.

"Open it!" Longarm ordered, shoving his gun barrel deeper into flesh and wrapping his left forearm around the man's thick neck to keep him steady.

The sheriff opened the door and there sat Judge Henson. He was fully dressed and held a nearly empty bottle of good whiskey in one hand and a pistol in the other. "I knew you'd come here after I heard you killed Ike and Etta last night," he said raggedly.

"Drop the gun!" Longarm ordered.

"Go to hell!" Hanging Judge Henson spat, lifting the pistol and pulling the trigger as fast as he could.

The judge's first two bullets smacked wetly into Sheriff Belcher's bare chest, and before the man could fire a third round, Longarm shot Judge Henson in the shoulder, knocking him over backward in his chair.

"Oh my gawd!" the night clerk cried.

Longarm let the sheriff drop in the doorway and moved inside to kick the pistol out of Judge Henson's hand.

"I'm bleeding to death, damn you!" the judge cried.

"Yeah," Longarm said, righting the chair. "I expect that you are."

"Help me! Call for a doctor!"

"Nope," Longarm said, tossing the judge's gun aside and smiling. "I hit you in the left shoulder because you're right-handed and you'll need your good right hand to pen a confession absolving me of all crimes and stating that you and the sheriff were in cahoots to have me hanged."

"I said for you to get me a *doctor*!"

Longarm cocked back the hammer of his Colt. "Are you ready to sign that now, or do you want to find out how bad it feels to lose a knee and then bleed to death while I go and have a few shots of good whiskey to celebrate?"

Their eyes met for a moment and then the judge nodded. "You win. Give me the pen and paper. All I ask in exchange is that I don't face the hangman."

"That will be up to a new and honest judge and jury," Longarm told him. "But if you don't sign a full confession right now, I'm going to shoot your knees and you'll bleed to death screaming for a mercy you damn sure don't deserve."

With a trembling hand, the judge grabbed the pen and began to write out his confession, and it was all that Longarm could do not to start laughing.

Watch for

LONGARM IN THE LUNATIC MOUNTAINS

the 386th novel in the exciting LONGARM
series from Jove

Coming in January!

LONGARM

GIANT-SIZED ADVENTURE FROM AVENGING ANGEL LONGARM.

BY TABOR EVANS

2006 Giant Edition:

LONGARM AND THE OUTLAW EMPRESS

2007 Giant Edition:

LONGARM AND THE GOLDEN EAGLE SHOOT-OUT

2008 Giant Edition:

LONGARM AND THE VALLEY OF SKULLS

2009 Giant Edition:

LONGARM AND THE LONE STAR TRACKDOWN

2010 Giant Edition:

LONGARM AND THE RAILROAD WAR

penguin.com/actionwesterns

M456AS0510

DON'T MISS A YEAR OF

Slocum Giant
by
Jake Logan

Slocum Giant 2004:
Slocum in the Secret
Service

Slocum Giant 2005:
Slocum and the Larcenous
Lady

Slocum Giant 2006:
Slocum and the Hanging
Horse

Slocum Giant 2007:
Slocum and the Celestial
Bones

Slocum Giant 2008:
Slocum and the Town
Killers

Slocum Giant 2009:
Slocum's Great
Race

Slocum Giant 2010:
Slocum Along
Rotten Row

penguin.com/actionwesterns

M457AS0510

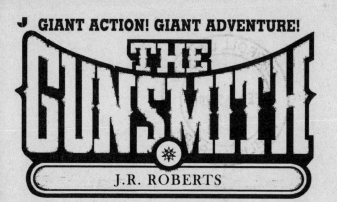

GIANT ACTION! GIANT ADVENTURE!

THE Gunsmith

J.R. ROBERTS

Little Sureshot And
The Wild West Show
(Gunsmith Giant #9)

Dead Weight
(Gunsmith Giant #10)

Red Mountain
(Gunsmith Giant #11)

The Knights of Misery
(Gunsmith Giant #12)

The Marshal from Paris
(Gunsmith Giant #13)

Lincoln's Revenge
(Gunsmith Giant #14)

Andersonville Vengeance
(Gunsmith Giant #15)

penguin.com/actionwesterns

M455AS0510

CARROLL COUNTY
FEB 0 0 2011
PUBLIC LIBRARY